NEIL CAMPBELL

SAYING DIRTY THINGS IN REGIONAL ACCENTS

SALT
**MODERN
STORIES**

**S
SALT**

CROMER

PUBLISHED BY SALT PUBLISHING 2025

2 4 6 8 10 9 7 5 3 1

First published in Great Britain in 2025 by
Salt Publishing Ltd
12 Norwich Road, Cromer, Norfolk NR27 0AX United Kingdom

www.saltpublishing.com

Salt Publishing Limited Reg. No. 5293401

A CIP catalogue record for this book is available from the British Library

ISBN 978 1 78463 333 2 (Paperback edition)
ISBN 978 1 78463 334 9 (Electronic edition)

Typeset in Granjon by Salt Publishing

Printed and bound in Great Britain by Clays Ltd, Elcograf S.p.A.

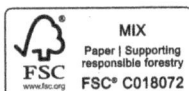

To Naomi, who can't be arsed reading this

Contents

Pugs Not Drugs

IT WAS HER that wanted the pug, but it was him who had to walk the little fucker, and there he was, every night, round the block, all bastarding weathers. The pug stopped and Butty stopped, the pug walked on and Butty walked on.

He'd never had a dog. Grew up around cats. All you had to do was feed them and then they kept to themselves. He'd have loved a cat. Fat fucking ginger, something like that. But no, she had her heart set on a pug, so what could you do? He loved Kaz and everybody had told him that marriage was about compromise. True that. The man compromises and the woman doesn't. Bob's your uncle. Bad a bing, bad a boom.

Another thing he compromised on was the time he had his tea. For years he had it about five, same as his mum and dad. Butty used to make it so he could watch the Paul O'Grady show at the same time. Now it was seven, sometimes half seven, and then after that it was time to walk the pug. And she called it Poubelle, god knows why, so there he was, out on the street, calling to Poubelle. He sounded a right knob. Ironic thing was, you had to fucking drag him out, every single fucking night. He didn't want to walk, and neither did Butty, and that was the little thing they had in common.

A happy wife equals a happy life. Too fucking true, and if you asked Butty, he'd say that was fair enough.

Better than the old life.

Crack On, Cocker

Lottery for me is a quid a week, every week since they started it. I've had a few tenners here and there, that's all, but come Saturday I'll be there watching those numbers roll. And of course, I've stayed with the same numbers, why would you want to change your numbers? Imagine if you changed them and the numbers from before won? How could you live with that? No, cocker, crack on, keep the same numbers, and one day your ship will come in and you can fill your boots. I'm waiting for that day, and when it comes, maybe on Saturday, I'll be out of here, I'm telling you, you won't see me for dust. I won't be like those tossers who win the lottery and keep their jobs, keep going to work. What's that all about? No way, you won't see me. But stick with the same numbers, cocker, stick with them numbers whatever you do. Thems yours.

Eighties Banter

THERE WERE THREE lads did the picking and packing and one of them was this old lad called Jimmy, he'd been there about thirty-five years, was a bit of a character, made the other two lads, Billy and Pete crack up laughing. Trouble was, it was often at her expense. All these suggestive comments. She came to expect it. Just banter. Boys will be boys and all that.

One day she was out there, having a fag near where they all sat on their break. Billy and Pete were sitting on boxes, eating bacon butties, and Jimmy was late for his break, so he said later. She'd seen him do the tripping up thing before, where he pretended to trip up and then bumped into people. Well on this day, he did the tripping up thing in front of her, but instead of just bumping into her he tripped and grabbed her tits. Billy and Pete were laughing their heads off and Jimmy was laughing his head off too, looking into her eyes as though to say, come on love, do something.

Dancing Shoes

Until this point, he'd been wearing these big black boots he got off his dad, and they stank, he'd had to wipe mould off the toes after putting them on and the laces left a stink on his fingers. But better that than dropping a flange on your toes and getting them crushed like what happened to Ronnie's mate, No Balls.

He was in the boozer when No Balls took off one of his Adidas and showed him these toes all bent to fuck, and No Balls told him, look, when you get that warehouse job first thing you make sure is you get decent boots, don't go in your fucking dancing shoes and expect to last five minutes.

With that in mind, Ronnie made sure to borrow the boots off his old man. And he had to wait ages to choose the new boots. You ordered them through the catalogue and they came within twenty eight days from this place in Northampton.

He was sat in one of the old wheelchairs in Goods In, listening to a Chris Rea song on the radio. Then the bell rang and it was a delivery driver and he had about six boxes of boots. Ronnie shouted to the other end of the warehouse and everyone came running down. They ripped open the boxes, pulled the balls of paper out of the boots and put the boots on. The foreman wandered down and watched.

Everyone put them on, and at first, they were going on about how great these boots were, but then after a bit, Ronnie noticed that everyone was limping around. He wondered why nobody said out.

Fucking hell, these boots are well uncomfortable, he said.

What did you say? said the foreman.

They're fucking murdering me these.

Look, some of these lads have waited a lot longer than you for these boots.

And?

Put your fucking boots on, all of you, and get back to fucking work, we've wasted long enough on this.

As the foreman walked off, he eyeballed Ronnie. Ronnie jacked the job in not long after and sold the rigger boots to a bloke in the boozer for twenty quid. He put that towards what he'd saved on the job and bought himself a quality pair of dancing shoes.

Faded Plastic Wristband

THERE WAS MORE in the car park than usual, and Mary was muttering even as she found a place to park. When she went in the bloke on the door wasn't so friendly, just took the three quid. She went up the stairs and into the pool area, changing as usual in one of the wooden cubicles. She glanced at the pool and it was filled with children.

The pool was childless by one bells and Mary dived in, coming up to the surface and breaking into a decent crawl. They hadn't cordoned it off for the proper swimmers yet, but Mary just went head-first for the shallow end. She hated it when they put the rope in, narrowing the pool down to about ten yards, and then put signs up with the arrows telling you which way to swim.

Swimming was easier on the old joints. She did half a mile each day. Thirty-one lengths. Some days she was quicker than others but she always tried to do thirty one. But it was hard to keep count when people kept getting in the bloody road.

When she'd done the thirty-one lengths she got out of the pool and used the key on the faded plastic wristband to open the locker. Then she took her stuff into one of the cubicles and got changed. As she put on her jumper, Mary looked across at the pool. There was a load of women in the water holding babies, the sun shining in on them through the glass roof.

Seven Volumes of The Old Cake Tasting Cunt

D ON'T WORRY, THE people will come, they said, so she sat there in the shipping container, listening as the rain fucking belted down on the metal roof. They put her chair in between classic fiction and poetry, so she only had to reach out a hand to find great words at her finger-tips. For the first four days no fucker came. Not one single customer. Then day five, it all went pear-shaped.

Day four and she'd just finished *Crime and Punishment*. Bloke kills one or two people near the start and then bangs on about it for five hundred pages. But then there was also Svidrigalov, or whatever the twat's name was, the devil himself. Charismatic bastard.

It was Saturday morning and she had just started on Proust. Seven volumes of the old cake tasting cunt. That would kill the time. Well, *Swann's Way* positively rattled along, she'd get through that in about fourteen fucking years, if she didn't hack off her own face first. She was just thinking about this when the doorbell rang.

Hello, good morning, young lady, said this grey-haired old bastard.

Alright?

Yes, I am alright. Erm . . . I seem to have got lost.

Oh yeah? Not a book lover then?

On the contrary, I'm something of a bibliophile.

I'd keep that to yourself.

Indeed. And when you say, 'round here', where exactly do you mean?

Look, where is it you want, chief?

. . .

Where do you want to go?

Erm . . . how to put this?

However you like?

Quite. Well, I mean, that doesn't matter now, perhaps I can look around.

Fill your boots.

I'm sorry?

Knock yourself out chief.

Yes, yes. Unusual set up you have here.

I'm reading Proust now.

Understood.

It was at the moment the old man turned his back on her that she thought about doing him in. She looked at the hardbacks. *Moby Dick*? No, she still wanted to read that. There must have been some other fucking hardback that would do the job. *Canterbury Tales*? Maybe that would do it. Cave the cunt's head in with Chaucer.

Down the Dancers

IT WAS AFTER one of these nights when he got home and he'd had a drink that Madison started having a pop at him, and he did what he thought was only right in those circumstances. He smashed her right in the fucking face.

He was only a little fella. People didn't get it when he said he worked as a bouncer. But when he fixed the stare on them, then they believed it. You could scare the shit out of people with a stare. And when he put on his long black leather coat, he looked bigger, and he always kept at the bicep curls. But it wasn't about physical strength, it was about what your head was like. Fight or flight. And when the pressure was on, he went fucking ballistic.

When he was a lad, he was sitting in Bigwigs on a Sunday afternoon. The strippers were on. He was only sixteen and he thought it was fucking great. And this fella and his Mrs were having a barney, and she had these big fucking painted nails and she scratched this fella right across the face. And what he did was he grabbed her in a headlock and started hammering her fucking head against the corner of the table. He did it over and over until a flap of skin was sagging from her head and she finally stopped trying to scratch him. And at the end of the night this fella and his Mrs went home arm in arm. It was the only thing these fucking bitches respected.

Thing was, the night he smashed Madison in the fucking face, she cleaned up in the bathroom, bided her time. When she came down the dancers he was slumped on the couch, laughing at the TV. He didn't notice her go into the kitchen for the big kitchen knife, but he sure as hell fucking noticed when she started hacking at the back of his head with it, over and over, in a fucking frenzy that, in the end, he stopped.

Every Single Letter
Holding a Sliver of Piss

WORKING FROM HOME was miles better, he'd never get pat and mick. But these colleges, loads of little scrotes running around coughing and sneezing everywhere, and the same on the bus, an hour there, an hour back. They'd tried to improve the buses by having air conditioning on them, but you sat upstairs and you couldn't hear from the noise it made and it just blew all the germs around the bus.

In the college as well, he had to go in different class rooms, log in on different computers. Can you imagine all the germs on those keys? Every single letter holding a sliver of piss, bacteria on every single key of the keyboard, words spreading germs from fingertip to fingertip. Then you went in the canteen and picked up a chip muffin.

As he waffled on at them about *Dracula* for the eighth consecutive year, he could see the vision in the corners of his eyes blurring. He kept drinking from his water bottle, hung on until the end of the class.

He struggled all afternoon, going through language features and structural devices with a bunch of listless fuckers who couldn't give a flying fuck about GCSE English. There was one lad. Pissed him off every week, so much so that Peter dreaded that class the night before and didn't sleep properly. Time after time he told this lad to put his phone away and time after time this lad refused. Every time he said something this lad questioned it. Now in some ways Peter thought this a good thing, tried to go with it, but the lad was just a little twat, there was no getting around it. Just a self-entitled little twat who'd never had to want for anything in his whole life. All on a plate for him. His parents had probably never said a single critical or negative thing to him, so he walked around like he owned the place. Good parenting, people. Peter hated people like that. All confidence and no substance. You could achieve so much as an average person if you did stuff with confidence. Perhaps it was his own lack of confidence that meant this touched a nerve so much.

He walked over to the lad and vomited in his face.

The Grabbing Bastards

THE BRUSH IS a heavy fucker, wide, and she grabs it and drags it out of where it's kept in front of the fire escape, flaps it down at the end of the goods in bay and starts pushing dust across the yellow numbers and boxes. There's a gust of wind from under the rackety shutter doors and it shifts the dust like wisps of sand dune in shadow. That's a bit too poetic, she's just sweeping up, does it every fucking day, its murder, hurts the back, the pushing and pulling of dust, one way and another into patterns, squares, long black heaped lines like distant hills. Jesus, enough of that, it's graft, pure graft, a whole day signing for boxes and lifting boxes out of the back of vans, then putting all that stuff away before half four if possible so there's time to spend sweeping up at the end of the day, so the bosses walking past that way to the car park and their big fucking cars can look and see what's what, because, don't worry, if there's still boxes on the floor or the floor isn't swept then the next day will start with the foreman having a pop and that will be the morning fucked.

Old bloke she used to work with always said, at the most depressing moments of the week, there must be more to life than this, but she always thought the old bloke was wrong, there wasn't more to life than this, this was life.

It becomes a mantra, the sweeping up, must sweep up, must get it done, drives her throughout the day, gets her through each day, each week, each month, and if she gets loads of overtime in then she's minted, it starts piling up in the bank, though it's never as much as she thinks it's going to be once the tax have taken their slice.

She buys a car from a second-hand place, young guy who seems to know his stuff. And the car means she can get up twenty minutes later in the morning. And then she thinks about the car, and all the cars on the car park, some of them here seven days a week, the grafters, the grabbing bastards, and where do they go in their cars, except to work?

Last Chance Power Drive

H E H A D T H E remote control in bed and so he put it on like he always put it on but unlike him I was not born to run. Every morning that same fucking song. In every room the posters, in every room a stereo with him playing. The Boss, Bruce, Springsteen, every fucking where.

And then the book came out. *Born to Run.* A fucking memoir. As if the album wasn't enough. So, Tim was there, every night in bed, reading from this book and going on and on about what a great writer Bruce is. So now he is not just a musician whose music plays twenty-four hours a day in this house, he is also a writer. Oh Charlotte, echoes of Kerouac, Tim said. Could easily have been a short story writer too, he said. Charlotte, you should read this, you must read this, he said.

And then of course there are the DVD's. The nightly DVD's of concerts from New York and Barcelona and Hyde Park, London. The guy plays three fucking hours, minimum. The DVD's seem at least that. Multiple discs. Behind the scenes. The making of. On and on.

For years, Tim spent loads on bootlegs. But now we

don't get CD's with shitty covers on, and music where you can hear people in the audience talking, we get downloads. Download after download, slowing down the computer. Gig after gig after gig. And it is always the same songs. *Thunder Road*, *Racing in the Street*, and *Born to Run*. The highway's jammed with broken heroes on a last chance power drive – I used to like that. Many moons ago. Now it's like having a boring shag.

Just after I first met Tim, at a Bruce gig at the Old Trafford cricket ground, it was a glorious summer evening, something of a rarity in Manchester. I wore a print dress and these boots I used to have, and it was too hot for a bra though I still don't really need a bra, and we danced together on one of the cheesy songs, *Waitin' on a Sunny Day* I think it was, and he held me from behind and pressed himself up against that thin dress I was wearing and it was thrilling and I was into it, the music made us sway together and it was so hot, so hot, there was sweat on him and he was my own Bruce, even if he couldn't dance, there was so much to him then, so much possibility, so much ambition, all the things he told me he was going to do, we were going to do, and that we never did. We don't touch so much anymore either and we never did have kids, we couldn't. But we got through that. For years, Bruce got us through the bad times, all those gigs we went to, so many gigs, the cricket ground again, the Etihad, twice, but now he is a reminder of those bad times, the music is like a chain around my neck. When he does new stuff, I will give that a listen. I like his quiet stuff but I also like it when he straps on the electric guitar and gives it some welly. And I love how old he is and that he is still doing what he is doing.

But all *our* lives, we've just watched what *he's* doing.

Before Tim met me, he had met Bruce. I'm sure that will come as no surprise to you. And he was always telling me about it. How he was going to ask for an autograph but just got someone to take their picture instead, a roadie or another fan or something, I forget. There was the picture of them together. It was in a frame on our bedside table. Both smiling, arms around each other, Tim towering over Bruce, and Tim isn't a big guy. So, you see, Tim was into Bruce before he met me, and me and Tim, well, we don't share anything that's ours, that we discovered together, nothing that compares anyway.

Bruce's face peers at me from the front of Tim's t-shirts. A t-shirt for every tour. It is a funny thing, but Tim has a beer belly and it pushes out the fabric of the t-shirts so that Bruce seems to grin widely at me from a fattening face. Tim goes jogging because of that beer belly. No shit. He isn't born to run. Far from it, fat twat. Coffee mugs have Bruce's face on. Key rings. Pens. Album cover prints in frames all down the hallway. Day in day out, his voice, his face all around the house.

This morning, what I did, I took the picture of Bruce and Tim out of the frame, and I put a picture of us in. It is from our wedding day. Outside Manchester Town Hall. Taken by me, not the photographer we hired, Tim's mate. An afternoon in early summer. We held hands outside and there were all these office workers around on their breaks, and I was a bit cold and Tim cuddled me. We carried on having our picture taken by the photographer, and we sat on a bench looking across Albert Square. Then we kissed again, and I took a selfie of us on that bench and that's the picture I've slid into the frame.

You know something, you know what *I* like? I like musicals. Bob Fosse. *Chicago, Cabaret.* And you know before that, Fosse was a dancer, a great fucking dancer. He did the jazz hands thing and used chairs and bowler hats like Fred Astaire. They think he used the hats because he was bald, but, wow, what a dancer. I used to be a dancer too, way back before Tim. They used to weigh us all the time. I hated that, that's a whole other story. But I loved the dancing. That movement, that fitness, being lost in the dance, all toned and not tired, never tired. Maybe I will dance again. I don't need Tim for that anyway. Charlotte the dancer. That's who I was. That's what I want again. Charlotte, that is my name.

No Places Left in the Care Homes

Don't panic, Sandra, he said, though that's exactly what was bloody happening, a panic attack.

Breathe, just breathe.

I can't . . . that's what I'm telling you . . .

I'll make you a cup of tea.

Ambulance.

Calm down, you don't need an ambulance.

I can't breathe, Brian, that's what I'm telling you.

Don't talk, he said, and put his arm round her. You need to get up, it will be better for your breathing if you stand up.

She stood up, and he was right, it made things better. She sat on the edge of the bed and felt better.

They went to A&E that morning and they told her she needed to be in hospital, so she stayed. They wanted her in for tests right away and she was put in ward 6.

The bed was near the window, six floors up. But people walked up and down the corridors all the time. Doctors and nurses kept checking up on her every hour on the hour, and she had to share the room. In the bed next to Sandra there was a woman called Marion.

When Brian came back in the afternoon, bringing her a James Patterson novel and her Kindle, as well as a box of Maltesers, this woman Marion walked over.

Has he come to kill us? she said.

This is my husband, Brian.

Has he come to kill us?

He's here to visit.

They all want to kill us, you know.

He's visiting me now, so if you could just let us talk.

Are you going to kill me?

. . .

Brian, pull the curtain across, said Sandra.

I'll press this button, if I press my button she'll come, the nurse will come. Why does everyone hate me? Marion said, picked up her walking stick and shuffling off down the corridor.

She's like that all the time, apparently, said Sandra. Nurse was telling me this morning. They shouldn't even really be in here. They need to be a in a care home, but there's no places left in the care homes.

Sandra began to struggle for breath.

Don't talk so much, love, said Brian, passing her the mask on the wall.

Marion came back, pushing through the curtains and staring at Sandra.

Why doesn't anybody care? she said.

Oh, go away, said Brian. Leave us alone.

Why don't you care?

Leave us alone.

Are you going to kill me?
Don't bloody tempt me.
Oh my god.

The Sally

CORNED BEEF LIVED under the Mancunian Way, in a tent alongside other tents, close to the campus for Manchester Metropolitan University. There was a conference on homelessness coming up, where well paid academics came from all over the world for two days of seminars and free meals. In preparation for the conference, Corned Beef and his neighbours had their tents removed from under the Mancunian Way. After each day of the conference, the academics sojourned to The Sally. The university owned the pub. But that hadn't always been the case.

When Corned Beef used to go in, there was a mix of students and Hulme locals, and never an academic in sight. Corned Beef and his porter pals from the town hall went on pub crawls in various directions outwards from the centre of the city, and the Sally was near enough on Oxford Road. Sometimes there was a poetry night on and the pool table got moved out of the way. If that happened, they wandered over to the Footage and Firkin. After a few beers Corned Beef was steady handed at pool and darts; a confident break builder and a quick minded calculator of doubles.

One night in the Sally there was a cocksure student in there taking the piss at the pool table. He waved around a sloshing pint, and bragged, I haven't paid for a frame yet! Corned Beef's colleagues stepped up and got beat and then it was Corned Beef's turn to rack them up.

This kid wasn't any good. He was just some bullshit toff keeping it real and slumming it among the working class. He never potted one off the break. So Corned Beef let him break. He split the pack nicely. Corned Beef eight-balled him without even chalking the cue. The kid wanted a rematch, but Corned Beef fucked him off, announced to his porter pals that it was time to be moving on.

Corned Beef had played pool since school, back when cool cat Mick Delaval had first given him the nickname. Keith, a.k.a. Corned Beef. Rhyming slang. No more to it than that. And now he had it in marker pen on the wall of his tent, in a new spot outside the central library.

Voyeurs

H E L O O K S A T his watch, switches off the TV, goes to the kitchen. He stands there, no light on, the blinds widened ever so slightly. Her light is on, but he doesn't see her there. Patience. He puts the radio on in the dark kitchen, listens to the evening concert, keeps his eyes on the window opposite. He goes back into the living room for the binoculars. When he comes back, he thinks he sees her, just as she's moving away again.

He keeps watching. Can she see him? He can't be sure. Anyway, would she do it if she knew he was there? She must know. Doesn't the light from her window shine on his, show him there in silhouette, his hand on the blind opening it still further? Does she see the binoculars? The light from her room shining off the lenses on them?

He keeps watching. He doesn't care. His girlfriend will be home later, after working at the pub. He's not some sad loser. He has a life, he will marry her one day. He loves her so much it scares him. A commonplace feeling. But this is the stuff of films. The stuff of fantasy. She isn't even that attractive. Not his type anyway. Attractive to someone else maybe. But she clearly has no boyfriend. Every night during the week she is in bed by nine thirty. In bed before the evening concert has finished.

He has put the binoculars down, so he can push the blind open with one hand, hold himself with the other. He hasn't even seen her yet, and he finds himself getting hard. It is the prospect of it, he realizes.

He tries to work out what flat she is in. He goes around the back of her building one afternoon and looks at the buzzers. Top of the building, must either be flat 5 or 6. That is the way with these Victorian conversions. His own is filled with damp, but the rent isn't bad and he loves being at the top of the building, having a view of the people walking by on the street.

He waits. She's there, passing quickly past the window. She has a mirror on the wall opposite. Can she see him in that, his shadowy hulk against the blinds, one arm moving just perceptibly?

She never looks directly out of the window towards him. That is when he realizes that she knows. Surely if she didn't know he was there she would do that sometimes? Look right towards him? She is complicit in the game. This doesn't spoil it for him. He isn't a pervert or a sad loser. He has a girlfriend and thinks this makes everything about him seem okay to other people.

One night he comes home at around nine thirty, realizes as much, and looks up at his dark window. Parallel to it is the kitchen window of the man in the flat next door. The tall, dark-haired single man next door.

The Bike of the Village

I WAS A wild kid, and when I got older, I thought back to certain incidents and adventures, dangers I'd put myself in, and bloody hell, sometimes I had to laugh. I liked that about myself, was never one of those ones that did everything by the book. Everything was so bloody boring growing up, especially in that school by the motorway. It was so dead there most people just went through it by car or the train, and the faster they went through it the better.

There was that cliché thing at parties of all the coats being on the bed. I had a clear memory of not wanting to do anything, of saying it, but feeling knackered from something more than Bacardi Breezers. And then I was awake and for some reason couldn't talk.

Waking alone there, the coats all gone, I knew this was more than a hangover, it was almost like blindness.

I realized I couldn't tell anyone, even though I was hundred percent about what had gone on. And the longer I left it the harder it got to say. They already thought of me as the bike of the village. His word against mine.

You saw it on the news often enough, women getting dragged through the courts and even if they win the case the bloke only gets a year or something. So that would happen, if we got the conviction, and it was a big if, but yeah, say we got the conviction, then after a year he's back in the village.

I went on cruise ships, all over the world. Caribbean, Greece, Cyprus, all the sunny places. What happened didn't ruin me, I was determined about that, and I drank as much as I wanted, wore whatever I wanted. That wasn't the problem. Sometimes there were men that were alright, like the one I almost got married to until he started acting weird. They always started alright, but I guess there was just something about me that changed them into arseholes.

The Hour Passed Like a River

Y OU WENT IN at lunchtime with the lads. Played darts and had a few pints. The cricket was on TV. Orange buses went past the window. The hour passed like a river.

Back on the forklift, the beer in you, floating around the warehouse, radio playing tunes of the time, tunes that take you right back there now whenever you hear them. Accidents, minor accidents, yes, they happened, but nobody was really hurt. The sun came in under the opening shutter doors, maybe there was a female driver there for once. When she left the stock got put away, no pressure felt, just a drift around the loading bay in a haze of harmless drink driving.

The afternoon wandered by and then it was a short walk to where the pub used to be, and with the sunlight still shining in through the windows more beer was had, pool was played, and before you knew it, maybe you'd reached Wednesday.

This was back before they changed the city by knocking all the old pubs down and reducing the red brick walls to rubble, before the cranes went up and tall glass buildings lined the sky reflecting the big dreams of little men.

Crayon Drawings

WHAT STRUCK HIM most was the sight of the lines on the door frame in there, where they had measured the girl as she was growing up; the sight of them and how they stopped at a certain height. He bent down to try and read the faded biro but couldn't make out the actual measurements. The lowest line was so low, the highest not that high, and he stared at that highest line before turning off the light and closing the door.

He went out into the back garden, looked out through the gate and down the embankment at a cycle path. A man cycled slowly down it, three young kids cycling in front of him, one still with stabilizers on.

He slid the rusty bolt into the lock on the gate and wandered through the garden, past a cracked greenhouse. He followed the paving stones towards the back door, weeds spiralling out from the gaps between them, went in through the patio doors, stood in the dining room.

He headed up the creaking stairs, the creak amplified without the smothering of carpet, and went into the main bedroom. There was a space where a bed had been, and a darker oblong of beige carpet than the faded beige surrounding it.

In the bathroom, he saw the mirror above the sink and the words still there for all to see. The toilet seat was down, the window slightly open, bringing in a breeze that fluttered the toilet paper hanging from the roll. There was a regular drip from the shower head, and a pattern of those drips in the bath.

He saw into the smallest bedroom. There were crayon drawings taped to the walls, a bunk bed in the corner, and on the top bunk a smiling teddy bear, tucked in tight under the covers.

A Bag of Cans on Stockport Viaduct

T HE SUN WAS setting as she crossed the road and walked past the boarded-up pub where they used to go, and into the car park and then through the fence and up the embankment, ignoring the warning signs and stomping out onto the pile of stones by the side of the lines. She walked up a bit, towards the station, and then put the bag of cans on the viaduct wall and climbed up onto the wall and cracked open a can and watched the trains. That's all she wanted to do, watch the fucking trains, but no, not in this day and age, fucking Orwell and all that, and these dicks in high viz walked over, aggressive at first, but they soon calmed down when she threatened to jump. One woman stayed and they waited around for a bit and she thought she seemed alright but then this muppet rocked up, started talking to her, and this muppet, it was just his training talking. Then the trains started slowing down and all these clowns started taking photos or filming it and some people shouted out of the windows for her to just kill herself, jump, go for it, get on with it and there were others calling her a selfish bitch for fucking up the trains. They started stopping all the trains and all she'd wanted was to have a beer and watch the trains for a bit, get a chance to calm down for a bit but no, they couldn't leave her alone, could they? She drank her cans and sat on there for hours and only got off the viaduct when the cans were finished. The trains had been in chaos, she found out later, but she hadn't been on the telly or anything.

Venables or Thompson

S OMEONE PUT IT on Twitter first and it seemed just like a rumour, but then there were photos and it was him, you could see it was him, okay a few years younger, but it was definitely him. And people said he was still into porn, had got done for it. How did he get the job working with us? That's what I want to know. I had to do work experience before they'd even give me a start here and he just came right here, was a manager pretty much two or three weeks after he started. Now I'm not one for gossip, me, and some people say you have to forgive and that's why we have the probation and all that, you give people a chance to change, but for me, personally, after what he did, I'd lock him up and throw away the key. It's like my mam says, some people are just born evil. You can see it in their eyes, like when they show you the mug shot from the police station, people's eyes always give them away. And how that mother coped with that, I don't know. If my Lauren ever went missing, I don't know what I'd do, but I know this, for me, I couldn't live with myself unless I tried to do something before the police got them. I'd do time for it.

I mean, none of us could work with him once it came out, once the rumour was out it spread like wildfire, and Greg, one of the other managers, he has three kids and he lost his job over it, he had this lad by the throat, calling him a paedo and all that. Now for me, I wouldn't lose my job over it, I was just going to ignore him, and if Greg had just left it a bit, he would have been okay.

Some days, like on my first shift at the start of the week, when it's pissing down or something, and I've got soaked walking from the bus stop, I feel like just jacking it all in and getting on a train somewhere with Lauren, somewhere new. I bet he could get a job anywhere he wants, and he probably will. It might be somewhere near you.

Patriarchy Chicken

L OOK I DON'T get angry about the man spreading, these guys don't know they are doing it most of the time, but the other morning this man's leg was touching mine with the movement of the train and he just kept letting his leg rest against mine. I moved it away and he'd ever so slightly move it over and then this man smiled at me and I said to him, loud, to his face, and with a smile, because I'm brave like that, I said, what are you smiling at? And this man went red and didn't say anything, I'd called him out. So I decided I was going to carry on with it, and I walked down the platform in a straight line, did not give way when men came towards me, and you could really see how it messed with their heads, the fact of me not moving, and then this big man just refused to move and wheeled his suitcase right into my legs, and then he was shouting at me to get out of the way and this other man shouted back at him telling him to shut up but I didn't need him to stand up for me and I carried on as I was.

I don't move to the side, I never move to the side and I've got bruises on my elbows, on my shins, but I'm not backing down against anyone and if I see that man on the train again and he does the same thing, or if some other man in a suit does the same thing then I will call them out again. Once I was on the train and this man was walking up and down the crowded train and he was rubbing against me when he went past, brushing quite deliberately against my chest, and you know that's not an accident, there's a lingering going on, and I didn't say anything that day because I was just in shock from it. Then yesterday I had this thing where this man stood there, about a yard in front of me, not moving, and he was just stood there gently smiling, like he was in love with me or something.

Vivaldi's Spring

Y OU GRAB A tea bag and pour hot water on it. After a while there's the regular interruption:

Thank you for waiting. Please continue to hold and we will answer your call as soon as possible. Or you may prefer to call back later. Our opening hours are eight am to seven thirty pm on Monday to Friday and nine am to four pm on Saturday. We are closed on Sunday.

After about forty minutes there's a live human voice on the other end of the line asking how they can help you today, and you tell them that you just wanted to call to say that it has been a pleasure all these years, but that now it is incumbent upon you to announce that due to a variety of extenuating circumstances beyond your control, it is likely that you won't have to phone them again.

Sentences and Fragments

EIGHT SENTENCES PER hour, written so slowly Phil could see the thought going into the curve and line of every letter. If Jack could fanny around smoking and getting a coffee until twenty past nine, then he'd do the eight sentences after. Without the fag and the coffee, you wouldn't have got the eight sentences.

The main thing about Jack was that he was a compulsive liar, did it for attention. First thing he told Phil was that his parents had died in a car crash in Canada, and that he had been adopted. Then he said his dad drove every morning from Wales, just to drop him off at college. He also said he and his dad worked for NASA, and, when a drone caused chaos at Gatwick Airport, he said it was his dad's drone.

Phil wished he hadn't read through some of the stuff on Pro Monitor, had thought Jack was a nice lad: inappropriate sexual comments that frequently upset Pauline, the previous support worker, fights in class, throwing a piece of metal at the tutor and getting chucked off the mechanical engineering course.

Phil sat there week after week telling Jack to be quiet,

or to get off his phone, or stop swearing. And the other lads in the Skills for Life class were funny. Compared to the mainstream classrooms he'd been in, where it was usually just mouthy little twats moaning about everything, he enjoyed it.

You just listened, built a rapport, acted as an advocate. The worst bit was the smoking shelter, standing in the wind and cold, passive smoking, guarding Jack's fags. Phil was on his phone so didn't really notice until it had happened, but one day a group of lads asked Jack to smoke a fag through his nose and he did.

Then, after preventing Jack from having the usual thirteen sugars in his mocha, Phil sat next to Jack in the silent classroom and asked, so, what are we going to write about this morning?

So tired this morning.

Well, it's twenty past already.

I told you before, I didn't sleep last night.

Why?

I was with me girlfriend.

Okay. Well doesn't she know you have to be up for college?

She's disabled.

Oh right. What's her name?

Natasha. You know something?

What?

You know something? I'm going to tell you something now, sir.

It's nearly twenty-five past.

Oh, shut up, I'm being serious, sir.

What? And I've told you, you don't need to call me sir.

I'm going to tell you something now.

What?

I love her. I love her with all my heart, sir.

That's nice, Jack.

I know. I'm a nice lad me. Aren't I a nice lad? Do you think I'm a nice lad?

Jack, you're a nice lad. But we need to do the eight sentences.

I'm tired.

Finish your coffee. Now, what are we going to write about? What plane haven't you told me about yet? What other planes do you make?

I don't know.

Well, have a think.

After a few minutes, Phil watched as Jack began to slowly write, his eyes right over the page, the pen moving slowly through the lines and curves.

Phil read through the first sentence. So, what's it called, a Swiss Miss?

Yeah, Swiss Miss.

Okay, so you've said it's a Swiss Miss. What else can we say about it?

Nothing.

Well, how about how long it will take to make?

Ages.

But how are we going to write that?

He picked up the pen, put his face down close to the page, began the slow process of writing.

Phil looked at what he'd written, corrected some of the spelling, and continued the laborious process of getting Jack to write eight sentences.

I need to phone my Dad up so he can tell me the size of the engine.

You shouldn't really be on your phone, Jack.

Phil watched as Jack picked up the phone. He didn't have any disciplinary powers, working in learning support in a college. He just sat there in the quiet and listened.

Dad? Dad?

What do you want?

Are you okay?

Yes, I'm working, what do you want?

I'm in college.

I know.

I'm writing. I've done loads of work.

Very good.

I'm writing about the planes.

Good. Look, Jack, I'm working, what is it?

You know the Swiss Miss?

Yeah?

What's the size of the engine?

I don't know, off the top of my head.

Can't you go and look?

It's in the garage.

Oh, Dad, can't you just go and look?

Right, give me five minutes.

Thanks Dad.

I'll call you back when I've found it.

Thanks Dad.

Okay.

Dad, can – Dad?

Doctor Morphine

(for Joel Lane)

H E DID SIX fucking people on our street, one bastarding street. Fucking hell, there's more coming out every year. I used to go in The Grapes, my old fella played bowls round the back, crown green bowls, not flat green, and he'd be out there in all weathers playing because he loved it and his dad, my grandad, played it as well. Not sure why I never did, I think he showed me once and I just couldn't be arsed with it. I'm not going to mention this cunt's name that did the six on the lane, he did fucking shedloads over the years and the police round here well you think they might have been better but there wasn't really the technology in them days. I watched this programme and it said he'd done the six and it showed more footage than I'd seen before, of him being interviewed and that, and him sitting with his back to the interviewers the arrogant bastard and that famous footage of him on TV coming out of the back of his place to talk and deny everything, and, seeing the relatives of one of the women he did, part of me wished I'd agreed to the interview, but that was ages ago now, TV takes ages to come on, doesn't it? It must have been like thirty years ago now, yeah, that's right, thirty years ago since it all came out, and what they showed in this programme is that he could have probably carried on but he got well cocky and fucked up. What he used to do was go round to the old dear's house and put the morphine in their tea, and then he'd go back, pretending to be on his rounds, and he'd find them dead and report them dead of just like old age or whatever. When it wasn't just old age he put on the death certificates, he had to make it more convincing, and they showed that on one of the ones from the lane here, what he did, the evil bastard, he killed her and then went back to the office and changed the medical records to make it look like she was ill when she wasn't even ill, and it was only because a computer expert at the time was able to see that he'd done this that they were able to build up the evidence against him. And he'd changed her will, so she left all her money to him, which was a bit of a piss-take really. I have memories, like my memories of my old man, playing crown green bowls. He was out there nearly every day after me mum had gone, but when they dug her up and found there was still the traces of morphine in her it seemed to just take the spirit right out of him. I can remember when he stopped and why he stopped and he lost all the mates he used to bowl with and he never got any exercise any more, he just used to sit there day in and day out watching TV, he loved TV my Dad, it was invented when he was a kid and it always seemed amazing to him and he had all these programmes recorded on the Sky box and he never got round to watching them all. That's where I found him, sat in the fucking armchair in front of the TV like he'd just fucking given up, couldn't be arsed anymore. I'd wanted him to be angry but he said he couldn't get angry and he was a gentle old soul and all he could ever do was beat himself up about the fact that he had defended the evil bastard, he'd said to everyone around that it couldn't be possible, it couldn't be true, and he felt fucking stupid, you were supposed to protect your wife weren't you? That's what he said to me once in a whisper, and he had this kind old face, breaks your heart to think about it, and me mum, well, me mum, I've not really said anything about her yet and yet she was the one got bumped off, one of probably hundreds they reckon, and she was the only person in my life who never let me down, even more so than my old man, she was just on my side at all times, whatever I'd done, and I'm no shrinking violet, let me tell you, I never was and then when I found out about her it sent me over the edge a bit you know, I got horrible after too many beers and I was always wanting to fight someone and it was the police I fucking hated then. By now I know that the police did make mistakes but there were others that did a good job, the ones that got him were fucking well dedicated, but I was looking for someone to blame and there was this one time that I was roaming round the boozers on a Friday night and this copper came up to me and said I needed to settle down a bit and I took a swing at him didn't I, didn't really connect but before you knew it there were four of them on me, and I spent a night in the cells at the same cop shop where the evil bastard got interviewed. They gave me a lift home in the morning.

Job and Knock

CHRIS DOES THE night shift because no other fucker wants to do it. So he deserves the better money and the fact that they can usually get the job done early doors. It's what they call job and knock.

Most of the lads are on the iPlayer all night, catching up on the football or *Line of Duty* or whatever. But they've been getting away with it so long they're even getting bored of the iPlayer.

Why don't we just go to the boozer for a bit, says Chris, to Phil, the lad he's on the job with. Phil can't come up with a reason not to.

Nobody ever mentions management. They're a joke anyway. Most of these night shift lads said could have got management jobs if they'd wanted but they couldn't be arsed with the hassle of going to meetings and all that, they just wanted to crack on with the job.

They started the night shift at six bells and by eight they went to the boozer. It was only about a thirty-yard walk from the exchange. Months they'd been dragging this job out, on and off.

They went in the pub and it wasn't like they

remembered. Instead of cosy corners and comfy seats it was full of tables and families sat there having meals. Screaming kids all over the place. Both Chris and Phil had enough of that at home. Part of the reason Chris did the night shift was that he got more kip on the hammock in the back of the van than he did in his own bed.

The pints cost a fortune and of course you had to go outside with your fags as well. Just wasn't the same. It was like they were deliberately trying to get rid of pubs for the drinker. They were just restaurants that sold the occasional lager now. This boozer didn't even do Guinness anymore. They always used to have great nights on the Guinness in there.

On the way back to the exchange they stopped at an off licence and picked up a four pack of Foster's and some fags. Back in the exchange Chris turned on all the lights and they flicked on one after another. They sat there at the tables and then Phil asked if Chris knew the way onto the roof.

Yeah, think so.

Better than being stuck in here. Let's have a wander up there.

They trailed up the stairs carrying the beer with them and went out through the fire escape and onto the roof. The bright lights of the big city stretched out before them.

Phil went back down and brought a couple of chairs back up and they sat there on the roof smoking and drinking.

This is fucking quality, said Phil.

Nice and cool on here as well. Boiling in that exchange.

Better get these beers down us.

Save a couple until tomorrow mate. No sense driving home pissed. One's enough anyway. It's like the fucking *Shawshank Redemption* up here.

Marching Not Fighting

B EEN WORKING FOR these jokers years now, all through the name changes, all through the management restructures. I had eighteen months on probation once for wearing the wrong boots. They gave you these work boots and they were well uncomfortable. I'd been alright wearing my own boots for fifteen years before that and nobody said anything. Then one day, back when I was on the poles, this twat straight out of uni comes along and sees me up the pole in the wrong boots. Doesn't say anything to my face, instead goes back and reports it. I tell you, if I hadn't have been in the union all them years I would have been out on my arse. They've tried getting rid of a few of us. The increments mean we're on shedloads more than the new staff they're getting in but these new lads haven't got a clue about fibre.

When they brought fibre in, fucking hell, what a stress that was. I'd been on copper for years by then and this was totally different. Bit stressful. We went on a training course in Ireland for a week and I've never drank so much ale in my life. One guy pissed the bed he'd drank that much. I finally got the hang of fibre though and been doing it years now, but you can't train these youngsters, they've got no attention span. You get put on the job with one of them and you try and have a bit of a chinwag but you can't, after five minutes they're on their phones. Then there's them out of the army. You think they'd be better at the job but they're not.

Best time was when I used to knock off early doors. Job and knock they call it. Everyone did it. I used to have the dog in the back of the van and when I finished the job, wherever I was, in those days it was usually the countryside somewhere, we'd walk in the hills all afternoon and I'd get home to the wife and she'd see how tired I was and she thought it was from the job but really it was from walking. I remember once she said how knackered the dog looked. She wondered how he could get so tired just kipping in the back of the van all day.

I could have sat the dog up front in the cab with me in them days. Nobody bothered. In them days one bloke even used to go round selling duty free out of the back of the van. This was before they put the trackers on us. Now the van is tracked I can't go for a shit without them knowing.

And they send us out all over now. This new system. It's total bollocks. They said it would be more efficient. So now I spend most of the time driving here, there and everywhere getting to the job and sometimes by the time I get there it's time to come home. It's not like the old days but it's easy enough driving the van. I have Radio 2 on. There's no dog with me now and I have to wear a high viz all the time but you know, if you're in the van you aren't working. Marching not fighting we call it. And you know something, I can't even get a decent signal where I am, it's a joke.

Slaughterhouse Two

H E WAS BY the pig farm, fiddling around with the strap on his walking stick, when he saw the two of them.

You alright lads?

Yeah, they both answered. One was a redhead, the other had curly black hair.

You off school?

We've left school, said the redhead.

Oh right. You'll have to get jobs now then.

We've got jobs, said the redhead. Here.

At the farm?

Slaughterhouse, said curly. Start next week.

Oh right, you looking forward to it?

Not really, said curly.

I am, said the redhead. Money isn't it? We'll get about one fifty a week each.

Curly hair asked what the man did for a job.

I'm retired, he answered.

There was no response from either of them to that.

Right, the man said, watching as they leaned against the drystone wall, I better be off. Good luck lads, he said, walking off with the smell of dead meat in his nostrils.

Black Like the Crows

THEY'D BEEN TO the park in the shadow of the high-rise and they sat in the park on the slightly damp bench and she sat there pushing the pram back and forth with one hand but the baby wouldn't stop crying. She knew it was winding him up the baby not crying and she remembered that Chekhov story she read at Uni where the woman ends up smothering her own baby but she could never do that.

A breeze blew off the river and there was the threat of heavier rain in the wisps of rain but they were out now, had to make the most of being out after being cooped up all day high up there on the fifteenth floor.

She sat on the bench and watched him as he walked off around the fields smoking one fag after another. There was a punctured football in the long grass behind the leaning back goalposts and she watched crows eating berries in the branches of trees like they sometimes did in haiku poems. As the crows ate the berries she watched as he kicked the football around the field towards the goal at the far end and when he got near the other goal he kicked the punctured football towards the open goal and missed.

When he came back the baby was still crying even though she had never stopped rocking the pram and he kicked one of the wheels of the pram and the baby cried louder. She looked across at the crows and they had multiplied, there were dozens of them crowding the trees until there were no berries left at all and the trees that had been filled with red were now black like the crows.

He wanted to go back, said he was cold and was sick of the fucking cold but she didn't notice the cold at all. She stood up and turned the pram round and they started walking down the footpath and the baby was still crying. The baby kept crying until they reached the green metal footbridge, where he threw it in the river.

Exposures

W HEN I FIRST moved in, my father's things filled
the flat. It took me a good two years before I could
bring myself to throw any of it out but gradually I started
taking it to the charity shops. Soon all I had left were
the paintings and photographs he had on the wall. I had
grown to like them, especially the photograph that was in
his bedroom – the one where the woman had an exposed
breast. And then there were the letters from his women.

I didn't love my father. Nor had I ever worshipped him,
not even as a child when you were supposed to. He never
kissed or cuddled me. He would pat my head. He never
spent time with me either – always away on business. I was
never quite sure what he did all those years.

I wondered how my mother had felt about the letters.
Had she ever seen them? Did she know about his women?

One day, I received a letter from a woman saying how
sorry she had been to hear of my father's death. The fact
of receiving an actual letter was strange enough, but how
did she know he had died? She also purported to have been
my father's lover – she said she could prove it. Had I ever
seen a photograph of a woman with one breast exposed?

Well that was her, she said. How could she have known that, I wondered? Did he take the same picture of all his women? Could you put them all together and fill a gallery with their faces?

We met in my favourite café on the corner of Half Moon Lane – I will never forget it – and though she had obviously aged I felt straight away it must be her – I'd looked at that photograph so often. She complimented me on my hair and skin and I felt at ease with her from the start. Her hair had turned grey, and it hung down in plaits, which she fiddled with all the time, unravelling and ravelling them.

We ordered another pot of tea and sat looking out of the window. My silence encouraged her to talk. It was like she hadn't told anybody anything about her life for a long time.

I'm sorry to tell you this, but I *know* I was the love of your father's life. I always liked your mother, she was good for him, got him off the drink, but with me he was wild, we had some wild times. Especially when we went to Brighton for the weekend. Do you know the Lido here? We got naked in there once and they threw us out. I was always taking my clothes off in those days. I had nothing to hide. I walk around my flat naked, even now. You should do it, it's a liberating thing.

I smiled, and she continued, there is one thing I would like to ask you. I am happy being old, I'm happier now than I've ever been. Since my own husband died, which was obviously very painful, I've felt a freedom greater than ever before. And because my mind is not what it was – I used to have a photographic memory – I find my memories falling away day by day. In many ways, that is a good thing, believe me, one forgets all the mistakes one has made. But

I'm losing the good memories too. So, what I would like to ask is, could you possibly let me have the photograph that your father took of me? The one you say is still on the wall in his bedroom?

I agreed, of course. It was of more value to her than me, though I liked the picture. It was a beautiful breast. Maybe that was what I'd always looked at, rather than her face. I said I would get the photograph for her, and we arranged to meet later that day, once again in my favourite café on the corner of Half Moon Lane.

When I took the photo off the wall I turned it to the light and saw the face in the picture more clearly, in a different aspect, and something about it troubled me. I dusted the photo – I had always been very poor at cleaning – and again I felt ill at ease. It was like the face was slowly emerging to me like an image in a dark room. I wrapped the photo in a brown paper bag and put it in my handbag and returned to the café.

She was already there when I returned, fiddling with her plaits, her face different, bright with expectation. I sat down opposite her, in the window, and passed her the brown paper bag, which she took off me with trembling hands.

Rainbow Puddles

O N A BEACH more oil than sand they skirted rock pools and drifts and knelt to scoop bits of plastic from the water. They slid over clumps of blackened seaweed and splashed their feet and got their feet black and then the rain got harder and blurred the rainbow puddles.

The sea was out there somewhere they knew it like an instinct and their legs kept taking them out further. Under the pier they played with the tangles of seaweed on the pillars and flung black pebbles towards each other and sheltered from the smoking rain.

Beyond the end of the pier, they kept walking towards the far horizon and could hear waves in distant crashes. One of them went in up to the knee and it was funny, and they lay on the oily sand laughing in the rain. Their footprints in the oil receded behind them and some got flooded and covered.

Dark birds flew above and around them before landing on the mud and skipping uncertainly across the sinking sands, their faces jutting. They kept walking away from the dark birds and towards the sea before the voices shocked them into stillness. Stood in their tracks and already slightly sinking they turned around. Where there had been oily beach there was now seawater swirling around them.

Bananas

D AD PARKED THE diesel Escort just off Platt Lane and the four of us walked down the back alley towards Maine Road. As well as me and Dad there was this bloke with bow legs I don't remember the name of, and his son, who had a tash. Dad worked with the bow-legged fella at a place called Oldham Batteries that did a TV advert in the 70s that said 'I told 'em, Oldham' . . . Terry he was called, that was it, Terry, wore jeans and shoes with Cuban heels on them and smoked like Dad. I don't remember what his son was called. That smell of Silk Cut, always remember that, as we squeezed in through the turnstiles and went and got a programme that Dad always gave me to read first. I needed a piss so went to the bogs. In those days you basically slashed against a brick wall while standing in a line of other pissing cocks.

We stood near the halfway line about halfway up the Kippax Stand, looking out at all the green of that massive pitch. The pre-match entertainment then was watching the physio boot crosses over for the keeper to catch and I preferred that, not like all the glitzy flashing lights and all that bollocks at the Etihad now. Other entertainment was Helen the bell, who used to ring a bell all game from the bottom of the North Stand, and there she was, blonde hair flowing, bell ringing. And there was the groundsman, Stan, and his minions, going around forking the pitch.

As usual it was a shit game, occasional bits of skill in and among mistakes . . . I'm probably spoiled these days with Pep's teams . . . and more often than not we didn't win the games in those days, but it was weird, a win was more of an event somehow . . . anyway it was so fucking boring that there were a load of people around us holding inflatable bananas, most of them like three or four foot long or something like that. When you looked around there was all these other kind of inflatables around, and in this game, when you turned around and looked back up the stand, you could see a giant inflatable Godzilla having a fight with a giant inflatable Alf. From memory Alf was something off a kid's TV programme but anyway these two inflatables were having a fight and I swear to you half the stand had their back to the game, roaring and cheering when one of these inflatables bashed into the other. I'm not sure what was going on, there was always the sweet smell of weed in the air but I think this was around the time that E's came out. The players must have wondered what the fuck was going on when there was all this cheering with nothing happening on the pitch. There was another cheer as this inflatable doll got thrown around, and she had stockings and suspenders on her and then there was a large cheer as someone burst her with a fag and then she went flat. She was still getting thrown around and then it landed on Dad's head and he laughed his head off and just threw it off. It was bonkers, all of it, but I kind of miss that these days with all the prawn sandwich brigade and that, all the corporate boxes. But you can still have a bit of a laugh in the South Stand, there's still banter at the Etihad. But I always remember the time me and Dad went and all he said was, it's not Maine Road is it lad, and we smiled at that because all our history was at Maine Road. I think of that every time I go to the Etihad, when I'm wearing his scarf that still seems to have a whiff of Silk Cut on it.

Little Victories

WITH STAFF CUTBACKS it ended up being just me and Pete working there and for the same wages we had to do security and a load of stuff that they used to employ others to do. It was a joke, really, they said the university had no money but thousands of fuckers turned up every year and there were big buildings going up everywhere.

In them days I was always out on the piss on a Saturday night, so every Sunday morning I walked through town to the uni with a pounding head. It was dead quiet but there was always piles of puke and broken glass on the street waiting for some poor bastard to clean it up. Every Sunday morning I remember looking through bleary eyes towards a stretch of river that wound it's way out of the city and thinking how great it would be to just fuck off on a boat somewhere.

One Sunday I was waiting at the back door for Pete to rock up. Soon enough I saw his big silver Mercedes coasting into the car park.

Morning, cock, he said.

Morning, Pete.

Not that bad, is it?

No.

Ha, ha. Good, good.

What have you got in there, I said, looking down at this big carrier bag he was holding.

In good time, cock, in good time.

I went upstairs to the library staffroom while he let himself in to his little cubby-hole under the stairs. I'd always wanted to see what he had in there but he never let anyone in and if you approached the door he'd stand in your way.

In the library staffroom there was a note on the door that said, *Polite Notice: just because food is left in here over the weekend doesn't mean it belongs to you.* I opened the door and took out a Muller Rice, Strawberry flavour and had it for my breakfast. I also made myself some tea. There was always this stuff called Karak tea, powdered tea, and I made myself a cup of that, four teaspoons.

There were all these crap magazines like *Hello* and all that shit and I perved on the women in them for a bit and then made my way out to the library floor. There was nobody in yet so I went on one of the computers and checked my emails, which I always did once a week in those days. There was no social media or any of that shit back then, but I did spend a stupid amount of time on the computers when I could have been reading books. Sometimes I went in one of the offices and watched a bit of Brazzer's but then an email went round about the inappropriate use of computers.

There were loads of trolleys filled with books that needed shelving so I made a start, first of all sorting all the books into Dewey decimal system order and then wheeling the fuckers up and down the aisles and bunging them on the shelves in roughly the right places.

At break time I was in the staffroom, lying on the couch after having eaten another yoghurt, and then I dropped off, nodded off for a good hour. Instead of making me feel better it made me sleepy as a fuck and I couldn't be arsed doing any more shelving when I got up. There were hardly any students in and those that were, were on the computers. I wandered downstairs looking for Pete, and when I couldn't see him anywhere I went and knocked on his door. I could hear the radio from outside and had to knock a few times before he answered.

You alright, cock, what's the panic?

Oh nothing, nothing, I said.

What's up with you today, cock? Not yourself.

It's fucking dead here.

Nobody in?

One or two on the first floor but that's about it.

Well don't worry about it. You're getting paid aren't you?

Wasting my fucking life here.

You're a young lad, plenty of time.

What have you got in there?

What do you mean, cock?

Just wondering.

Nosey fucker aren't you?

Not really.

You want a little peak into paradise with Pete the porter?

Eh?

Come in, he said, opening the door to his little cubby hole under the stairs.

I walked in and there was this tall lamp in the corner with a posh red glass shade at the top of it, sending a red glow onto the walls. Beneath the lamp, with a copy of *The Sunday Mirror* spread out on, was what could only be described as a chaise-longue, or whatever they call them, made of red velvet. Next to that was a bedside cabinet, with one of them old fashioned teasmade efforts on it. There was a little fridge, another table with a TV on it that had an aerial sticking out, and then on a ledge next to the little oblong of frosted window there was one of them Roberts radios and it had the football on, commentary on a United match he was listening to. In the corner of the same table there was a kettle and a toaster and a teapot and a red tea caddy on it that said *Don't Let the Bastards Grind You Down*. There was this big fuck off rug on the floor and a little hoover in the corner and then best of all was this three-bar fire. It was fucking roasting in there but he still had a dressing gown on over his porter's uniform. When he opened the fridge door you could see it was rammed with beer.

Have a bottle of Pils, cock.

Might as well, cheers, I said, as he unfolded a deck chair and passed it over to me.

Hair of the dog that beer.

Yeah, tastes good.

Sunday tastes good, cock, Sunday tastes good, remember that. You had many in?

No, it's been pretty-

- oh, hang on, yep, Rooney's got another. Good lad.

Just saying, it's dead. No point in us being open.

Ours is not to reason why, cock. Anyway, going to be open twenty-four hours a day soon.

Why?

It's what the students want, isn't it?

United scored again and we drank our beers while listening. I stood up and adjusted the deckchair so that I was almost horizontal to the floor, then lay back down it, necked my beer and fell asleep again.

When I woke up the whole room was full of cigar smoke, and it was like a sauna in there and with all the smoke and the red glow of the lamp on the walls it was like being at the match when someone lets a flare off.

Time to lock up in a bit, cock, he said, as I got up. You might as well go home.

Cheers, Pete.

See you next week, cock, he said.

Oh, by the way, what's in the bag?

You're fucking dying to know what's in the bag, aren't you? Come over here cock, he said, little victories, that's what it's all about, little victories.

The Room

I T WAS A while since last time so the girl showed him part way up the stairs then gave him instructions how to find the room because obviously she couldn't be arsed going all the way up the dancers so he had to find his own way and soon enough he didn't know where the fuck he was there had never seemed any logic to the room numbers and then finally he found room 54 opposite room 39. There was one of those big orange vacuum cleaners just left on the floor outside but there was no cleaner around or anything but thankfully it was an old hotel and just had a key so you didn't have to fuck around with a fob that didn't work and that you had to take back downstairs to get swopped for another one.

It was an all right hotel, 4 stars and that and his room was well posh, he lay down on the big old bed and looked around and there was a bedside table and lamp thing all attached to the wall and a massive telly on the wall directly opposite the bed and a desk with some fancy paper and a pen like he was going to sit there writing letters or some such nonsense and on another table there was a little kettle and a couple of teabags and sachets of coffee and you didn't get much by way of teabags these days he'd probably have to go down and ask for more of them later. He got up and took the kettle to the bathroom to fill it up with water yeah fill it right up it's their energy bill, fuck it and he made himself a cup of tea with one of the PG tips triangle bags not his favourite a bit weak they were and he made it and put the tea on the bedside table and then with the remote he'd got off the desk he stuck the telly on and it was only Freeview with all the channels with a shit picture but that's what you got in the middle of nowhere, so he was stuck with the BBC channels and he left it on the local news, daft fucking accent the bloke had on there but it was a change and after his tea he got up and started running the bath, leaving the TV on and the water pressure in the bath was shite it always was in these old places but eventually the bath filled up and he got a little round soap packet and unwrapped the little round soap and lay in the bath enjoying the heat of it, felt his face going red so he leaned right back and submerged his head and came up dripping and when he got out of the bath with the big white towel around him he was chilled out as fuck all toasty and warm and wandered back over to the bed to read through the booklet for the evening meal and he wasn't really hungry and it was all a bit pricey so he just lay back on the bed and nodded off with the telly on.

He didn't know what fucking day it was when he woke up or even where the fuck he was for a minute and the telly seemed to have turned itself off so that was okay but there was bright light from somewhere shining in the window so he got up and dragged the thick curtains closed and got a glass of water from the bathroom and lay back down on the bed and realized what it was that was different, there was this constant droning sound coming from beyond the walls somewhere and he was wondering how he would get back to sleep he would have to, but what the fuck was that anyway? He could go down to reception but there wouldn't be anyone there in the middle of the night would they? Anyway he wasn't getting up and getting dressed and going down to reception so he just got back under the heavy duvet and tried to get back to sleep, and for ages he couldn't but then he did, only to wake once more and find that the drone from beyond the walls had turned into a roar, all the walls were roaring around him and he lay on his back with his hands covering his ears and the roaring was still there in the walls all around him, and now it seemed to come from above and below as well as from the sides and all he could think was why would they put him a room like this, why? What had he ever done to them?

He got up and put the key in the door and tried turning it but it wouldn't turn and he pulled and pushed at the door standing there in his underpants and he felt the sweat pouring off him and dripping on the thick carpet that even now seemed to get thicker and thicker sucking him down into its shag so that he felt like a man in sand, sinking sand but this was a hotel room how could this be happening, a hotel room in the middle of nowhere and then he saw the walls shifting to the side and all the time the roaring was going on and then the walls seemed to fall down, covering him so that finally he passed out.

Wet Patches

H E WAS OBSESSED with this dehumidifier, cost hundred and sixty odd quid and he was fucking obsessed with it, said we'd been living in a damp room all these years and that on the telly it showed this young kid in London somewhere had died because of the mould in their flat so we needed to get it sorted as soon as. I was like, how much is it going to cost with all the energy price rises and that and he's like, your health is more important and so I went along with it even though the smart meter was going higher than it should have.

It was a nice flat and the landlord Duncan was a good fella, only lived round the corner so if you had any mither with anything he could be round in ten minutes, not like some of these other landlords. In the last flat I had this guy lived in the fucking Peak District so if you wanted anything done it would take forever. So anyway, this flat is nice but the bedroom is cold because there's these big sash windows and a high ceiling and with the sash windows there's a gap of fucking fresh air halfway up where the wind blows in like fuck so we have a draft excluder on top of there. We used to have two sets of curtains on it but one day I looked at the lining in the curtains near the window and it was black with mould so now we've got just the one set of thermal curtains on it but it's the outside wall that's bad, before we had two wardrobes in front of it, not flush to the wall because you never put anything flush to the outside wall and then after a few years I looked at the back of them and they were thick with mould, so we had to drag them out and get it off, it wasn't like black mould this was just a layer of grey stuff and it brushed off the back of the wardrobes like dust and when my husband saw that he panicked like fuck and bought this dehumidifier.

There's nothing against that big outside wall now because we put the wardrobes over on the other side of the room but if the light hits the white wallpaper right you can see the wet patches on it, and there's bits where when you touch the wallpaper and it bubbles out and that, it's all loose on the wall and I'd been coughing my guts up, always just had a cough all winter and like I say this flat is fine and that and you can't fault the landlord it's just our bedroom gets damp, and I have to say, though my husband bores the arse off me talking about it, I have stopped coughing as much. This thing has got an air purifier on it as well as the dehumidifier but you should see it, we have it on twelve, eighteen hours a day, and there's this container that holds the water and you just slide it out and it's a great design and every day he's tipping pints and pints of water down the sink and I'm thinking, what if we both didn't have half decent jobs, what if you was on benefits or disabled or something and you didn't have the money to fork out hundred and sixty quid for one of these things, never mind to pay the electricity bill from having it on all the fucking time, I mean, how would you manage, and that kid in London that died from it, fuck me, what's happening to this country?

I bet if you're one of these posh cunts you're just thinking, why don't you just move to another flat, well, it's not as easy as that with the price of renting going up and up all the time. We can't afford to move anywhere else. This landlord only puts our rent up about a fiver a year and that's lucky for us because you can't get a one bedroom for less than about eight hundred a month these days and we just wouldn't be able to afford that.

Thing is though, the husband is pissed off because he keeps saying that the humidity isn't going down in the bedroom. Problem is that when you have two people sleeping in it at night and breathing all night it goes right up again, but what he doesn't know is that most afternoons Duncan's here as well.

The Pink

I WAS RUNNING to the shop like always because I'd got all this energy and then I was at the shop and just standing in the shop in a line with all the other blokes. They'd be taking the piss out of Greg as usual, asking if he was married yet and he got wound up Greg you could see it, he went red in the face and all the blokes knew and especially the reds. If the reds had won and City lost then they'd wind Greg up for fun and talk about Fergie this and Fergie that and Fergie time and the old Irish bloke on the counter just leaned there smiling and yawning. We'd all be looking out of the window and nobody talked to me. They knew I was just there to get *The Pink* for my Dad. The games used to finish at 4.40 in them days, they didn't fuck about at half time then like they do now. I remember when someone just booted the ball high into the air and to nobody in particular, because they wanted to waste time because the team was holding on for a win or draw, people called it a 'twenty to five ball'. Anyway, it would be about half five in the shop and we all stood there looking out of the window. Then, pretty much always at the same time, the little yellow and black *Manchester Evening News* van turned up and the bloke came out with all the newspapers wrapped in string. He came in the shop and dropped the bundle on the counter and the old Irish bloke snipped it with the scissors and started passing them out and taking the money. There was this big rush to get in line and get *The Pink* first and as soon as everyone got theirs that was it, they just fucked off, rushed out of the shop and went home.

On Saturday night, Dad would sit on one end of the couch, in the corner of the living room, with a lamp on behind him, *The Pink* spread out across his legs, and a can of lager and a quarter of ordinary peanuts on the table beside him. Though the TV was on all night and all the rest of us would be watching *All Creatures Great and Small* or *Hi De Hi!* or *Casualty* or whatever it was, Dad would just sit there, reading *The Pink* from cover to cover. This was every Saturday night without fail. There was this one time where he went to Market Rasen with work and there were strict instructions for me to go out and get *The Pink*. He had every copy of *The Pink* for years and years and they're all still in the loft, must be a right fire risk up there but none of us can face it yet.

Dangling Keys

I'D SEEN HIM in the Co-Op while I was doing a bit of last-minute shopping, saw him smile at me, then he was right behind me down one of the aisles. I took my shopping round the back to the car park, stuck the bags in the boot and then sat behind the wheel looking at a couple of texts on my phone. Next thing I know this fella is there right next to me, holding this big bottle of blue liquid, says he's got all this windscreen wiper fluid spare and I can have it for free if I want it. I look at him for a minute because I'd been reading the texts and all that and I was like well, I don't think I need any to be honest. And he says, standing there right next to where I'm sat in the car, he says, I can have a look under your bonnet for you if you want, and I say again no I'm fine, it's fine. And I'm wanting to get home and it's getting dark and I've had a right day at work and I just want to get home and he's like, you might as well have it and I'm like love, I'm good, I don't want anything, I don't need it, thanks for the offer but really I'm fine and then like out of nowhere he's like raising his voice, I was just being nice to you! And remember it's getting dark and that and I've not started the car, the keys are just dangling there in the ignition and he looks at the keys and says just let me look, there's probably a lever on your passenger side let me just have a look and I'll get the boot open for you and I'm like no love, leave it honestly, I appreciate the offer but I'm fine and he stands there he's all red in the face holding this wiper fluid and looking all pissed off and in my mind I'm like I need to get out of here and this guy's going on, that's the problem with you lot and then all of a sudden he's okay and smiling and he says, it's alright don't worry I'm fine.

Saying Dirty Things in Regional Accents

I

I N BED WITH a curly haired comedian, I was giving everything I had with my head between her legs, seeing more clearly where I had to go since she'd shaved down there. At no point did she do anything for me other than allowing me to shag her and then before she got in a taxi home she said thanks, you were number thirty-seven.

Before my early forties I was fucking useless with women, and that's a long time to be useless. I'd been to an all-boys' school and most guys I knew from there were still pulling their puds well into their thirties.

Because I'd never been around them, women became this mystical, wonderful thing, something special, and it was only when I met Andi while working at a call centre that things changed for me. She told me to treat women the same as men and that men and women are just the same. That was mind blowing to me and it worked. Instead of getting all nervous and trying to think of what to say to a woman I just spoke normally. By this time, I was already in my mid-thirties. It's ridiculous I know, but it was true. Sometimes I wonder, apart from occasional wanking, what the hell I did for all those years. In the really bad times, I would rush home from work and put a porno video on in my bedroom and pull one off before tea. Those porno videos were well grim, the tape all worn at the same bit, so that you knew, at the moment you shot your load, that that was where all the other sad bastards had shot their loads.

Women are well horny in their forties. They're divorced from sexless marriages and rampant for sex before the menopause kicks in. Around that time, I was seeing this woman Chris. She used to ring the buzzer of my flat all times of the day and night and most of the time I'd ignore her. Not because I was deliberately trying to make her more annoyed and horny, but because I genuinely couldn't be arsed.

I don't think I have a big sex drive to be honest. Those early barren years meant that I got used to living without it. For a while back there I reckoned I averaged about a shag a year, and now I'm more than happy if I get it every few months. There's more to life than sex after all. Also, it means that whenever I do get sex, and this was true even during the salad days of my early forties, I always shag with a smile on my face.

What brought those halcyon days of my early forties to an end was not just being listed as number thirty-seven in a young woman's shag pile. I also knackered my back. Years of not getting any, coupled with a tragic diet, meant that I had a weak core, had never in fact had anything resembling a six pack. I'd had a muffin top for as long as I could remember. But during that golden spell I was putting my back under tremendous strain. One woman, Georgia, wanted me on top just pounding her as hard as I could and this was great for a while, I even saw the beginnings of a six pack. Then one night as I was in mid-thrash it felt like someone had crashed a cricket bat into my coccyx. I squelched back out and remained there on all fours, getting no sympathy whatsoever. I made my way slowly to the bathroom, my hands against the wall the whole time, had a piss and then slowly came back out and put my shorts on. I had a road bike at the time and wheeled it home in the early morning sunlight to the mocking sound of blackbirds.

Jess is a really successful comedian now. I watched some of her act on YouTube but all she talks about is sex. The sex she has is research for comedy and I didn't even make the routine. I guess there are worse ways to live your life but it all seems pretty soulless. It's the kind of well observed comedy that makes you smile.

It was a funny thing, the day I met my wife. I mean, Sam doesn't even remember it the way I do. Wasn't love at first sight, that's bollocks. It was more the vibe I got from her. I don't know how to say it more than that. It didn't feel like a big thing at that moment. Within minutes we were taking the piss out of each other.

2

I don't want to go on about it but I reckon the main reason I hardly had a shag in my twenties and thirties was that every time I went out I got pissed. I loved to get pissed back then. Still do, now and again. What I do now though is drink a bottle of Merlot while cooking nice grub in the kitchen. I drink it while chopping onions and all that, and I have headphones on listening to Chrissy Hynde.

I loved beer as well. I mean, the taste of it, as well as what it did to my head, and when I thought I was in love with this woman I worked with I was so down on myself that I never even told her. I was stupidly shy and felt I didn't have anything to offer and I wasn't brave enough to get rejected so I drank beer. I went through this daft charade for years. I'm not sure if I loved Allie or not. Women that I might have had a chance with came and went. I just liked the way she was. I think maybe I didn't love her and was just charmed by her every time she fixed her brown eyes on me. She had a charm with people and I mistook that charm for more. She was nice to everyone. I still dream about her sometimes. It's stupid. I should have asked her out, got knocked back and moved on. The world is full of wonderful women but I didn't know that then so I drank, sitting at bar stools in my twenties all hunched over and acting like a deep sadness was driving me to drink because that's what I'd seen men doing in films.

3

For years all I ever knew about women was based on their tits or their arse, the way they looked anyway. I was around this kind of objectification all the way through school and well into my work life. You might think I've been objectifying women throughout this, but it's not that so much as the objectification of women being an integral part of my early adult life. Don't throw the baby out with the bathwater.

As a kid I played football and when we went on the team bus to away games it was a thing to just shout things out of the window to every fit woman we went past, and I joined in with it because I thought they might think I was gay if I didn't.

The first real time I fell in love the woman looked nothing like any woman I'd fantasized about from porn. Jo was great and I fucked up big time because I didn't know how to deal with the fact that she loved me.

When you're loved you're on this pedestal and you can never live up to it. After a night on the piss I got up the next morning and sent Jo a text telling her that I didn't want to see her anymore because I needed some space. Three months later I said I'd had my space and she told me to fuck off.

4

Second time I fell in love for real was with Sam, and after two years of taking the piss out of each other part time we moved in together so we could carry on the banter seven days a week. That's when the relentless shagging took permanent toll on my back. Thankfully things slowed down on that front not long after we'd moved in together and the workload became more manageable. Sam became my best mate, made me laugh more than anyone I'd ever known.

5

In the text message Sam said I had become almost entirely self-absorbed, and she didn't feel like there was room for any other voice in my life anymore. Blindsided, as they say on the telly.

I'm back to occasional wanking again. But at my age things are different. I tend to try and do it in the shower because the mess gets washed away. The other day I almost fainted from the effort.

Thing is, I don't do porn anymore. I find it unpleasant the way the guys shag the women so aggressively, choking them and all that horrible shit. I wank from memory and there's a lot of good memories.

What really works best for me is imagining sex with all the women I fucked up with, and generally it comes down to two women that I think about, and the memory is more about how they talked, the accents they had, and I think about them saying dirty things to me in their regional accents.

At the moment they keep showing this advert on the TV about erectile dysfunction and I switch over immediately. The more I see it the more it worries me. There's a mate of mine has been using Viagra for years, he says it's good if you really want to 'put on a show'.

Years ago there was a billionaire Texas pensioner who married a young blonde, and she would just stand by his hospital bed while he fondled her knockers. I think I'll just get one of them showers with a seat in it.

Toil

TWELVE DAYS IN and the sales were through the roof and all that. Bill looked around at his workmates lolling in their chairs but still looking at their screens and typing away. They'd brought food in for the weekend and everyone got a brown paper bag with a sandwich and a bag of ready salted and an apple and a carton of orange juice and a cherry flapjack in it. Last year they'd got pizza.

Bill clicked quickly onto the BBC sport page to check the football scores and City were already three nil up, Haaland getting a hat trick before half time and then being subbed by the great Guardiola, then he clicked back out of the page and back onto the intranet.

The thing was, after twelve days there was nothing left to say and Bill was an introvert, had always been an introvert, nothing wrong with that. In reality he didn't like people that much, they drained his energy. He needed time alone, usually at the weekend, or else he couldn't go on being nice to people, even if he wanted to be. He didn't see how he could ever go into management. These fuckers on the phone, do that, do this, I want this, I want that, I want it tomorrow, I want it now, fuck off. There's people starving and all that and you don't even know what to spend your money on.

About four bells this young lad Ollie starts juggling in front of his monitor, three little black and silver sacks getting flirted up into the air one after another. He says he needs to relax, he's got a stiff neck and this is how to do it. It's magic, he's like a circus act twirling these sacks around and around. Everyone starts watching and everyone starts having a go. For a minute or two all the ringing headsets get ignored and everyone thinks well fuck it we've met the targets and all that. But then Joe turns up, the big boss, and he's built like a brick shithouse and everyone thinks Ollie's going to get bollocked. Joe stands there and it's like he's about to shout at everyone. Then his eyes change and he's smiling and he says give them here, let me have a go and he picks them up and he starts juggling the sacks. Then he picks up an empty cup and he's juggling that at the same time as the three sacks so that's four things he's juggling. Everyone's amazed and then he puts them down and says right, back to work. Bill looks at him and thinks, wow, now that's management.

Cupboard Love

DOT RUNS THE Dettol wipe across the bottom of the emptied cupboard on the landing and leaves the door open for it to dry and then that's that, another job done. The dining table is full of plates and cups she'll take to the charity shop tomorrow. She goes into the pantry for the box the lad put in her boot outside Pets at Home and takes out a sachet of one of the fish flavoured ones. She empties the sachet into a clean bowl and all the time he's bloody miaowing at her. She didn't even want to keep the cat, now she's driving to Pets at Home and feeding it every day. Bloody cupboard love, that's all it is. She can barely get it into the bowl before he's got his head in there.

She checks the patio door is locked and checks she's got her keys and checks she's got her phone even though she has no idea how to use the thing. She goes out and locks the door behind her and gets in the car and takes off the wheel lock and puts on the radio. It's George Ezra, she likes him, they play some of his songs at the line dancing. She whizzes round to the off licence where she gets her four cans of Carling and a bag of the Walker's crisps, cheese and onion ones, and whizzes back again, no tootling along at thirty.

She gets back and parks where there used to be two cars. She gets in and can't see him anywhere, where's that bloody cat, he's normally all over her when she gets back. Bloody mithering cat, ties you down, you can't go anywhere. But he's nowhere to be seen, maybe he's run off. She puts her coat up on the almost empty row of brass hooks above the radiator near the front door and takes her shoes off and leaves them near the radiator and changes into her slippers. Already it's getting dark, she might as well batten down the hatches, so she goes and checks the patio door is locked again and pulls the curtain across most of the way making sure not to block the cat flap. There's still no bloody sign of the cat, and she goes to the front door and does the mortice lock on that and then goes and sits down and sees what's on the telly. Now her lad's shown her how to use the iPlayer there's plenty to watch. She's seen almost all the Shetland ones, is up to series 5 so she'll stick one of them on. Then she remembers that she needs to go and close the cupboard door on the landing. It's best to just do it when she remembers so she heads upstairs, one hand on the rail. When she gets up there, she can see that the bloody cat is sat inside the cupboard. It makes her smile, and it feels like it's the first time she's smiled since it happened.

The One Minute Barrier

*O*KAY, OKAY, JUST *take your time, you've took the top off it earlier, it's going to be a good un' this time, just take your time, take it easy, go slow, no rush, relax* . . . Right . . . right . . . oh . . . erm . . . oh . . . yep..yep.. I'm in . . . brace yourself . . . oh jesus that's nice . . . no, no, it's fine, it's, oh shit, don't do that, just hang on a minute, oh fuck, just . . . no . . . it's okay . . . okay . . . oh yes, jesus, fucking hell, *think of something else think of something of else, Billy Connelly said the eight times table, eight eights are sixty four, what are eight nines? Eight nines are, whoa* . . . aaagh, jeez . . . . . ok . . . ok . . . it's fine . . . fucking hell . . . *it's fine, just slow down she's loving it, you want to do this for her or else she's going to fucking leave, oh jesus but it feels so good, how can anything feel so good?* . . . oh for fuck's sake, for fuck's sake, *squeeze the base of it they said that'll stop it, are you fucking joke* . . . aaaaaaagh, jeez, fuck oh fucking hell . . . fucking hell . . . let's just stop for a minute . . . . okay, okay, turn round, let's, yeah, yeah, that's it, just turn over let's . . . .okay,okay . . . let me just . . . okay, yep . . . no . . . just . . . that's it, oh that's it, yes, I'm in . . . brace . . . ohhhhhhh fuuuuuuuuuuuck . . . Fuck. Oh fuckety fuck, Shit, oh fuck

I'm sorry it's happened again, oh fuck oh fuck, oh shit, what? Wait, I didn't hear what you said . . . that was over a minute I reckon . . . progress in my book . . . where you going love?

The Ticket

THEY WERE IN the café in the shadow of the town
hall and the town hall was all white and covered
up because they were renovating the Gothic. They were
sitting there and her face was set, he remembers that, set
like she'd made her mind up. It felt mad to him that it was
over and that they were both there in tears when if she
could have just moved on from it they'd have been fine.
But yeah, her face was set, she didn't smile at his jokes and
when he wandered towards the tram in St Peter's Square
it dawned on him that yesterday she'd known. That had
been a last shag with him and she'd made more noise than
ever because she wanted their last shag to be great. It was
like he'd moved on from that, he felt more deeply for her
now than ever before, right at the time she'd decided to
end it. He reckoned it wasn't anything to do with what he
thought it had been about at all and that was just a premise
for her to end it. She'd just probably found someone else
to shag and was bored of their shagging. That wasn't how
men and women were, that wasn't how they told you men
and women were. As he's thinking this he gets asked for
his ticket. He doesn't have a ticket and he tells the guy

fucking hell mate I've just split up with my girlfriend. They give him the big fine, they must get something out of that beyond just having to do it as part of their job, they are so hard faced. There's an old woman on one of the seats behind him and she says to her friend, that's not fair is it, he's just split up with his girlfriend. He's always remembered that and felt thankful for that bit of fucking empathy. He got off the tram at the next stop and walked it home past her house. He vowed never to speak to her again and after about two years of emails and texts and her blocking him from her Twitter and her Instagram and sending a threatening reply mentioning the police, he finally fucking accepted it and stopped wasting his life.

The Shortage of Black Suits

H E's SICK INTO the bath and washes it away with the shower and looks at himself in the bathroom mirror, his hands resting on the sink and shifting the sink slightly so it seems to shift away from the sealant on the tiles. He lifts one hand off the sink to his face so that it looks in the mirror like he's trying to hold his face on, stop it falling off, and there are caverns under his eyes and his eyes are piss holes in the snow, fag burns in a sheet. Where he had a chest he now has little tits but his belly's not too big, puking will do that for you. He washes his face, brushes his teeth, gargles mouthwash, puts moisturiser on, mainly either side of his nose where it's red, and he looks again at his watch. He puts on the black pants and the white shirt and the City blue tie. And then he puts on the black rain mac that he got from Slaters when they said there was a shortage of black suits as a consequence of COVID.

He sits downstairs on the bus until he starts feeling sick again and tries upstairs, opens all the windows and there's the rank smell of weed that seems to be all over these days when there used to be just some scrote at the back with a fag. Fucking hell, the bus is bouncing over every pothole, and he feels every bump in the road and at a certain point he just has to get off, so he gets off and vomits across the broken glass of a bus shelter on Dowson Road. He stands upright and gets his bearings and wonders should he wait for another bus, thinks no, might as well walk it, it's not far, and a few minutes after, when it's as far to walk back to the bus stop as it is to keep going, the rain comes, and the yellow bus comes splashing past, the white headlights bright in the puddles. At the next bus stop he thinks of getting the bus but then thinks he might as well save the money. The fresh air might help too. He's got a proper rain mac on anyway, should have bought an umbrella as well, he's never had an umbrella and never saw his dad with one either.

Outside the church there's lots of different people huddled in different groups under umbrellas waiting for the coffin. When the hearse turns up, he sees his brothers and some of his dad's mates from the pub. They have to wait a bit for the service in the church to finish and then three of them either side pick up the coffin. One old geezer nearly falls over from the weight of it, but he rights himself.

He watches and follows from the back as everyone filters in and nobody says anything to him. He stands at the back of the church and watches the service, his two brothers both losing their shit and collapsing in tears during their speeches, saying how great dad was and how everybody loved him and how he was such a great bloke, and that was right. He guessed it was too soon, maybe would always be too soon for people like him who'd fell out with his dad and never got back on speaking terms. Petty fucking grievances.

At the end of the service, they are playing that old Kinks song where they sing thank you for the days. He can see his mum at the front of the church. She walks up and stands next to the coffin in front of everyone and starts singing along to the Kinks song. It's the bravest fucking thing he has ever seen.

Maybe now his dad has gone, her husband has gone, maybe he can just talk to his mum again, spend some time with her before they were all here again looking at her coffin. It would be too fucking late by then, better to try and talk to someone, get to know someone before they died because he'd never fucking known his dad. Even when they'd got on, they'd never had a proper conversation. It was just banter and god he hated banter. What a waste of time all that was when you could have been talking properly. As he's thinking this, his brothers catch sight of him and stare and he realizes he'd better get the fuck out of there and so he does, back out into the pissing rain where his still-wet rain mac gets battered by more rain. He dives past some huddled smokers into a pub he's never been in before, has never really been round there at all except for funerals. The door is wedged open so that the smoke from the smoker's drifts in and the pub smells of smoke like it would have done all those years his dad smoked in pubs. It was fucking daft, if his dad was here now he'd still be adamant that smoking never did him any harm. He was the kind of bloke you could never disagree with, but he was his dad and now he was here in this pub without his dad. When he walked down the street he'd have no dad and when he called his dad on the phone there would be no answer. To be fair, there had been no answer for years now.

He remembers one time when they'd gone out onto the back fields where all the houses are now, when they'd gone out there and had a kick about. It was a Christmas when it snowed, and they all went out and played football on the back fields in the snow with an orange football their dad had bought them. He went in net between two trees and dived everywhere in the snow making loads of saves and his dad called him Big Joe after Big Joe Corrigan, the City keeper in those days. He would always remember that, when his dad called him Big Joe. He wishes he could remind his dad of that now as he tastes the pint of lager. But the lager tastes like shit, there's no hair of the dog going on here. He makes his way back out into the rain between the smokers all huddled in the doorway. He's not even decided where he's going yet, just starts walking.

Racks

H E WAS WALKING past the library or where the
library used to be and it was just all boarded up.
They'd got rid of most of the libraries now. As he sat in
the park he started thinking about when he used to go in
there as a kid. One time he'd nicked a load of boxing books
and his mum saw them in his bedroom and made him take
them back, so he sneaked them all back in except for the
yellow Muhammad Ali one. This was in the days when
they stamped your books with the date on for taking them
back. He was thinking about that as he sat there in a park
that had once been quiet but that was now roaring to the
sound of the cars and lorries on the nearby M60. He looked
around at the changes in the place and remembered he'd
have to walk under the motorway to get home.

He rearranged his blue and white scarf so that it covered
all of his throat against the cold. Looking at the disused
building where the library used to be, he remembered how
warm it was and how his love of reading had started there.
He also remembered how he got music cassettes by the
likes of Jimi Hendrix and how sometimes the cassettes
from the library chewed up your tape player at home so

you had to take them out and wind them up with a pen and how you could see the creases and folds in the ribbon.

He remembers as well, the one time he was in there and this middle-aged woman worked there and she used to wear jumpers with just a bra on underneath. He remembers one time just looking at her through the racks for ages and ages. There was nobody else in that bit of the library and with it lovely and warm with the big radiators and the sun shining in through the windows he stood there hard as fuck just looking at her grey jumper for ages: the wobble as she stamped a book, the way she stood with one arm on the counter, the one time she leaned back and stretched. He was so hard and it felt so nice just rubbing his dick against his leg. By the time he walked out of there his bollocks were aching like fuck.

No Longer the Best Mate

H E'S NOT HERE yet, what the fuck is going on? I look at my phone and there's a message on WhatsApp and it's like sorry mate something has come up can't make it this year but if you want me to book you the ferry as a foot passenger I can do that for you and I'm like what the fuck is this? I reply to him because I've just got up and I can't believe it, this is my one fucking holiday a year, I don't swan off all over like he does with his wife. I reply to him on What'sApp that I'm fucking sick of this, I knew this was going to happen, I don't know what I ever did to that wife of yours but she never wants you to come, every year I've been expecting this, and I tell him to fucking cancel it and there's no reply for about an hour. Then there's just one word of a reply that says cancelled and that's it I've never spoke to him since.

This is a guy who I first met at school when we were about 12 or 13, second year it was and because of the alphabet we were sat next to each other in Mr Hemp's German class and we got chatting and his brother was into cricket like I was and after a bit he started bringing in his brother's cricket books for me to borrow. So I began looking forward to that class, not for *wie heisst du* or whatever, but for borrowing these cricket books. During the lesson we'd be in a conflab over them and we were sat on the far left of the classroom and there was a bookshelf with a glass front and I'd stand the cricket books up in there so I could read them in class two pages at a time. This was like, what, forty years ago now? We've known each other ever since that, gone to test matches and I went to his wedding and he came to mine though his wife never came there was another fucking white lie about that.

You know what it is, do you know what I reckon it is, I reckon his wife has anxiety or something and he just can't leave her sometimes and that's what it is. I bet that's what it is, that's why he has to lie, that's why he can't fucking tell me the truth. It's some fucking pride thing or he's embarrassed or she's embarrassed or he wants to keep it quiet or something but because he doesn't tell me that I'm just like, well, your wife never came to my wedding and she fucked up my holiday and I don't ever see my best mate anymore so what the fuck do you expect me to do?

The Dead Bug

S HE'D BEEN AT the uni for a while, the first in her family
and all that, first from the whole of Beswick probably,
first and fucking last thanks to the tuition fees. She was
going to set up her own business that was where the money
was she wouldn't have to give anything to the uni anymore
she'd get it all herself though she'd have to rent somewhere
and she had her eye on this place in Spinningfields it would
be a big step but she was thinking about it when this bloke
Jonathan came for his appointment and said he'd had a bad
back for years and that he got it from work and so he was
looking for a massage to get it sorted and she explained she
didn't do massage this was sports rehabilitation so she could
identify what the issues were and he didn't look happy
with that she should have realized then but he changed his
fucking face and gave her a sickly smile and already she
knew but she carried on that was the job and she felt him
watching her, just her and him in her little physio room
with the table and the charts on the wall and the skeleton
in the corner and then she showed this guy the exercises:
the tabletop knee drop, the hamstring curl to bridge, the
dead bug, he was the fucking dead bug, and she could feel

him watching her and when she looked up from the floor at him more than once she saw his eyes on her arse and she gave people two or three weeks it needed two or three appointments to get them on the right track usually and this was the kind of thing that put her off, even if she got her own business and was her own boss she'd still have to help out these creepy fucking middle aged men with their dodgy backs and wandering fucking eyes and she'd had enough of it, fuck physio, then she thought why should I give up my career because of these creepy fucking men and after the latest sad fucker had left she went out, got out of there and ran through the streets of Hulme where men perved on her again and she ran faster, no headphones, just running fast and thinking of ways to stop men being so fucking horrible all the time and messing up her life. She thought maybe if you just didn't look at them looking at you that would help but why should she have to do that, it was them that needed fucking changing not her and she ran faster, her trainers slapping the pavement.

Sod That for a Game of Soldiers

S o HE's IN there and they ask him why do you want the job and he's like well, why wouldn't you give me the job, I'm great me, the dog's bollocks and you wouldn't regret employing me I mean yeah I got sacked from my last role but that was just circumstances and there isn't the time here to go into that but I mean it wasn't like the other job I got sacked from I mean to be fair I deserved to get sacked for that, twatting someone, but yeah I think you should be free to express your views on social media whoever you work for and er, yeah I wasn't going to mention the criminal record but you know I think it's best to be honest and that was a long time ago, anyway I feel like I'm waffling, why do I want the job well, why do *you* work here? I mean, I'm not being funny but would you work here if they weren't paying you? I mean I'd much rather stay at home and just mooch around all day but that's not going to pay my rent and they've had enough of me at the benefits office they really want me to get back into work so you know if you can give me like ten hours a week or something that'll get topped up by Universal Credit and then everyone's a winner I mean the thing is I only live round the corner, I can walk here in ten minutes or so that's a big carrot for me to be honest and I can start, well . . . I'm busy next week but the week after, I'm happy to start then but I mean obviously we'll have to talk about the money side of things, what's the money going to be? I mean is it going to be worth my while getting up early doors, I mean that's another thing, I'm not an early riser as such so we'd have to talk about that an all, I mean, Jesus, I can't be doing with getting up before about nine bells at the earliest, especially in winter, when it's all dark and that. Sod that for a game of soldiers. Anyway, when do you want me to start?

Man Lying Outside the Savoy

HE WAS IN the middle of the road slowly getting across, he should have gone a bit further up and crossed at the . . . he's getting across and can feel the cars either side of him slowly sidling forward, slowly coming at him from both sides and he stumbles . . . almost falls onto the road and finally lifts his feet one by one up onto the kerb and it's so fucking hot he can feel his red face is burned and his whole body is fucking clammy with sweat in fucking September for fuck's sake, why is it this hot he's thinking as his legs wobble and one gives way and . . . the other follows and slowly slowly he's heading down to the pavement and then . . . it's the pavement and the pavement is warm too but it's a fucking relief to just be lying there . . . if he can just lie there for a bit he'll be fine but there's people walking past all the time people just walking past a man lying on the pavement, lying in the fucking street and they don't care and he doesn't care he's happy lying there and then he hears this married couple walking past they have to be married the way they are bickering like fuck he knows the score and she's saying we can't just walk past and he says just leave him and she's like no I can't and they've

half walked past him when she turns back and she picks
up his little rucksack that must have fell off his back and
she puts it down next to him and she says are you alright
love and he tells her he's fine he just needs to lie down
for a bit and then she says have you taken something and
before I can answer she's like we can't have you here . . . and
then there's these others turn up and he can hear all these
voices and it's like because she stopped to look at him now
everyone's looking and it's like something from a fucking
film when he looks up there's all these faces looking back
at him and before he knows what's happening he's being
moved and the woman's like we're just moving you into the
shade love and they shove him into the shade and he can
smell the chips from the chippy and then someone gives
him his rucksack and the woman gives him some water in
a plastic cup and tells him to drink the water and he realizes he's right by the side of the Savoy cinema . . . fucking
architectural masterpiece . . . not that anyone notices . . .
and he sees lots of young women and girls making their
way into the cinema and he can see in the side window it's
Barbie that's on . . . Barbie the film . . . and he thinks well
that's fair enough . . . fair enough . . . you can't have me
lying in front of the cinema like that can you . . . it's not
like I'm . . . well . . . whatever . . . bunch of twats.

Gardens of Portway

FIRST THING MONDAY I get my coffee from Costa and then after I've sat in Costa for a bit where they all know me I head over to the Forum and go in the library. She knows me in there as well, all I have to do is go and sit at the table near the counter and she comes over and brings all the papers. I sit there reading the paper because I'm a man of culture me but I also like to have my finger on the pulse of what's going on. But really I just read the sports pages I can't face the rest it's just too depressing. Then I wander around the Forum and then before I know it it's time to make my way home. When I get home I stick the kettle on for a brew, I prefer tea in the afternoons and I look at the letters that have come that morning and I can see they are all from the housing association. So I don't even open them, they will all be the same letter, they are useless there. I just leave them on the floor, because I know it will just be about the garden again. Now my dad loved his gardening, but it's been about a year now, hard to believe it's been that long really. He was a proper horticulturalist, really looked after the place, the Alan Titmarsh of Wythenshawe he was. It was nice out there, all trimmed privets and an immaculate lawn and lots of lovely flowers in the flower beds either side. When he went I meant to keep it going in his memory but I just didn't, I think it reminded me of him too much. He was always out there in the garden, his knees on this padded contraption. He'd sit out there in a deckchair smoking a tab and surveying his kingdom. Once I'd left it for a bit it was impossible to catch up, everything grows like wildfire in summer. So now the privet hedges are all huge and ragged and patchy and the lawn has weeds all growing out of it and it's like up to your waist. The irony of the council sending me a letter to sort out the garden is that when the council had the money they offered to do the garden and dad was like no, thanks lads, I'll look after it. He said that because he could do a better job than them. You could tell with what they did in the houses either side, they just came along and mowed the lawn and it didn't matter if it had been pissing down they still mowed the lawn so that it was all mud. I know where these letters have come from, it's the clown that lives at the back of me here. He says the privet hedges are blocking his light.

I was in the garden last summer and he's coughing at the bottom of the garden. I get up and walk down the lawn and make it about halfway to him when he's like, I can imagine it's not been an easy time for you, but I'm just wondering about the privets and I'm like, let me just stop you there. Not been an easy time? Not an easy time? I think what you are trying to say is that MY DAD IS DEAD. HE'S DEAD. And this clown just walked off.

Bowls

H E'D ALWAYS LIKED Dylan, like the Best Of, stuff like *Changing of the Guards* and *Gotta Serve Somebody* but as he looked at all the CD's in his Dad's office he saw loads of stuff he wanted to listen to like The Waterboys, Roxy Music, Glen Campbell, China Crisis and The Icicle Works. He piled them up ready to take them home. He sat in the office chair, opened a drawer to the meticulous files, saw the jack, the white jack from crown green bowls, saw the little bowling bag with the bowling balls in, remembered the time his Dad had shown him how to play. They'd always had the bowls, fucking hell, they'd always had the bowls. I'll come back later for the CD's, he thought. When he did, he stayed in the office for a bit and found a newspaper cutting about the time his Dad had lost the Ken Mercer trophy, 21–19.

Chandeliers

M ATE OF MINE, when his wife left him, he wanted
everything to be new. New music, new films, new
places. A fair bit later he met someone new and he made
a joke of it to me, said he was shagging her off the chan-
deliers, jumping off the wardrobe, all that kind of thing.

Crates

MONDAY NIGHT AND she is waiting on the last one in the 7–8pm slot. She's just got rid of this guy who had been sat in his car on his phone while she waited with his crates of food. She was just stood there and he knew she was stood there and he was just on his phone. After all that she almost gave him the wrong crates, that would have been a right pain in the arse.

She stands under the awning. The sunset is pink. Two crows sit on a metal barrier. Over on the left there are three taxi drivers nodding off in their private hire cars. Closer, there are the teenagers in a car that seem to be there every night, and every time she looks over they seem to be staring back. Still, it's better than being one of the delivery drivers. There's estates you don't want to be going to at night.

The pink sunset is gone by the time the last car of the day turns up, almost right on eight o'clock. Little red Fiesta. Middle aged guy, always listening to Tina Turner.

Boot's knackered, he says, opening his passenger side door. He says this every time.

Okay love? she says.

Alright. How's your day been?

It's my last week this week, thank god, she says. Here's your frozen.

Got a new job?

No, no, I wish. I'm going to Australia for six weeks.

Oh right, he says, filling his carrier bags.

Yeah, can't wait. You've got no substitutes, she says, carrying over another of the green crates.

Great.

Nice one love, she says.

Whereabouts in Australia?

Melbourne. My sister lives out there, she says, putting the last crate on the floor near his passenger side door.

Sounds good.

Can't wait.

Cheers, he says, passing her the crates that she stacks on top of the others.

The guy shuts his door and starts the car, *Private Dancer* coming on again as he drives off.

She looks across the car park at the crows on the metal barrier, then over towards the taxi drivers, but they've gone. The teenagers are still staring over at her from their car. The crows fly off as she walks over there.

Footprints

There's just enough of as gap between his mum's car and the car next door so he reverses in and before he can get to the front door his mum is there opening it.

Before you come in have a look at the garden, she says, you remember those seeds we put in? Well look at them all flowering now, that's nice isn't it? The rest of it is a bit of a mess, I think I'm going to have to start paying a gardener to come, I say gardener, it took long enough for the bloody window cleaner to get back to me. Anyway come in, do you want a brew?

Yes please, he says, taking off his coat and sitting in the roasting hot living room where the TV is playing a James Martin cookery programme. The volume is so loud it seems like everyone is shouting and when she brings the tea in, he asks her to turn the TV down, which she does, to one setting below where it was before.

Did I tell you about the footprint?

Don't think so.

Well, I was in the back last week and I noticed this bloody big footprint on the table. I'm just sitting there with a brew and I saw this footprint and it made me worried because as you know we've been burgled enough times. Anyway, Ken next door has got CCTV so I asked him to look at it and he invited me in and I went and looked at it, you know he looks at it every day? Well we looked and it was the bloody window cleaner, wasn't it, I'd only forgot to leave the back gate unlocked for him so he'd climbed over to clean the windows. I'm so glad Ken has the CCTV because that would have worried me, you know?

Yeah, yeah. Didn't you notice the windows had been cleaned?

Well yeah kind of but I didn't put the two things together, I probably should have, shouldn't I?

It's good he's got the CCTV.

Well yeah it just stopped me worrying, so I'm grateful for that. You okay with fish for your lunch?

Yeah, I don't mind. Don't make a fuss.

Breaded haddock. With potatoes, corn on the cob and salad. Is that okay for you?

Great.

Now, do you want your salad on a separate plate?

I don't mind, mum, honestly, whatever.

Ok.

Is there anything else on the telly?

Put whatever you want on. Do you want another brew, or a biscuit?

I'm fine mum, honestly, he says, taking off his jumper.

Roasting

THIS GUY COMES round and I meet him in the library, that's what they do now they come to me. He gives me the new appointment at the end and I'm like, unless we can do time travel I don't think that's happening. He looks back at me all puzzled and it's because the date he's put on it is for a month ago. He's like, oh I'm sorry we're just so busy these days and I'm like it's fine, don't worry, and he's so stressed this guy he doesn't know what day it is.

I don't get stressed anymore, I've simplified everything, I'm at the library religiously every day until about four and then I come home and get my scarf and woolly hat on. I hardly use the electric and I got them to cut off my gas because I wasn't using the fire or the central heating. It was funny I got a letter the other day from the electric and they're like hello, we can't help noticing that you haven't put any credit on your card for a while and if there's anything they can do to help.

You know Jacamo, the clothing company? Well, they've give me this credit for clothes so I've bought a new coat and a woolly jumper and my woolly hat and all that and I don't think they realize I'm never going to be able to pay it back. But they keep giving me credit. I paid them a little bit back last month and so they extended my credit. They must think, oh well he's paying it back, let's give him more, so yeah, I get all my warm gear from them and I'm used to not having any heating on now. In fact, I'm fucking roasting most of the time.

Sold Out City

M ICHAEL WAS SWEATING cobs, the blazing sun cracking the flags and glinting gold stars off a line of azure skyscrapers as he headed into The Deansgate. After a swift Guinness he made the short walk to The Briton's Protection wanting to recall old times in there before they shut it down. He sat near the bar at a gold leaf table, looking out through the front windows at office workers scurrying past squinting at their phones and yellow trams dragging slowly to and from St Peter's Square. Walking out of the Briton's he turned left, heard the banging and clanging of building work, saw himself and the white walls of the pub dwarfed by the skyscrapers, skyscrapers a marked contrast to his own flammable high rise. He changed his mind about going to The City Road Inn, instead turning around and heading for The Peveril of the Peak. He relaxed further at the sight of the lime green tiles of the Pev walls shining in the sun, got himself a pint of Manchester Blonde and went and sat in the corner near the pool table, calmed by the shade and a cool breeze sidling through the open door.

Soon enough it was time to head back to work, but he

decided to extend his lunch hour indefinitely. That morning they'd been doing what were called ghost allocations, and in the way of admin that was an interesting title for a boring task where repetition burned you out by Friday. He'd been gagging for a drink all morning and with another pint of Manchester Blonde furthering his ability to sit in the corner of the pub on a Wednesday afternoon doing fuck all, he lolled back and emptied his mind and just watched the world before his eyes, absorbing, without his usual pre-occupations, what was going on around him. His phone was switched off to the bin-fire of social media and buried in his pocket. Nobody could contact him today, even if they wanted to, nobody. Nobody knew where he was, nobody knew what he was doing and the freedom of that cooled him further as he gazed around the pub.

There were four blokes in their fifties sitting in silence and slowly sipping their pints while trying to think of something to say, until finally one said that nostalgia isn't what it used to be. Right beside him there were two young women playing pool. They both wore high heels and their little fur coats were scrunched up on the seat together and they both had a lot of make up on and hardly looked old enough to be in there. One of them seemed less shy than the other while the shy one could barely look past the pool table as they bashed balls around trying to make the frame last forever.

This old couple stinking of fags came in off the scorching street. They must have been in their early sixties, breaking the relative calm of the boozer with their back and forth bickering and the increasing volume of their Prestwich drunkenness. The goatee man was holding a whisky and his blonde-wigged wife was moaning over and over about it being five quid for a double whisky, five fucking quid for a double whisky, daylight robbery and goatee man ignored her, they'd been together so long the ignorance was amicable, and he went to the jukebox and put on *Light My Fire* and started thrusting his hips towards his wife who told him to piss off, her eyes glinting with more than just the booze.

Michael looked at the women playing pool and the less shy one, the one with coal black hair and brown eyes, kept looking over at him, revealing a not too subtle amount of cleavage as she bent over the pool table to take another deliberately wayward shot. The other woman, peroxide blonde and azure eyes, showed just as much cleavage without bending over, but she didn't carry it as well as the other, wasn't as confident with it, was too young. Michael noticed that neither had a drink, just two empty half pint glasses on the table by their phones. One phone had a pink phone cover, the other was purple with pink stars and he felt flattered that they were smiling at him until he twigged. He couldn't really believe such things still went on on Wednesday afternoons in town, it was like a touch of the old town, but of course stuff like that was still happening all the time if you knew where to look. Soon they gave up on him, and everyone else in the old man's pub, and carried their fur coats back out into the boiling sun.

Michael moved on to The Temple of Convenience, stopping off in The Salisbury before heading finally to The Lass O'Gowrie, perhaps his favourite of the old Manchester pubs still standing. Massive black towers shadowed this old boozer now too, the tiny trickle of the Medlock beneath student accommodation for thousands, with thousands, not too far from the apartment block where Reynhard Sinaga stalked out to pick off his victims. It was dead in the Lass and there was a copy of *The Metro* on one of the empty tables. He picked it up and read about the ongoing scandal of the cladding, years after Grenfell, dodgy cladding that was on the outside of his own apartment block and on loads of others around town, where snide developers exploited the dreams of grafters. It had been going on for years, had cost him a potentially life-long relationship with a remarkably intelligent woman, and drained savings he'd worked his nuts off for.

He'd have to go back in work. He'd call in sick tomorrow, he couldn't just walk out of his job, but earlier that day he'd just wanted to forget it all. When he was in the Briton's he'd looked at the trams, thought of the trains, thought just get on something and go away and start again, disappear to the Lakes maybe, be surrounded by water. But he was bought into his flat, death trap that it was, and it needed sorting, it just wasn't right. As with Grenfell it seemed like no fucker cared, and whether you were in London, Manchester, Birmingham or wherever, you'd paid good money for a fucking tinderbox.

He walked home in the wrong direction at first, lost among the new buildings, the shadows of glass towers over everything and the CCTV everywhere to capture any life left. You couldn't even piss in the open air these days. He'd like to piss on some of these politicians and put them out.

When he finally stumbled in, he put the kettle on for a brew and then fished into the fridge freezer for something to eat, found some bacon in there for a butty. He ate the butty washed down with half the tea and then headed to bed, leaving the grill on and the bacon fat catching fire. The security officer on duty was long ago asleep, exhausted by her Law studies, and the flames began to streak up the dodgy cladding still nobody had agreed to replace. Soon the flames could be seen from the indifferent skyscrapers multiplying across the skyline. The emergency services, fallible in the past, thankfully got their arses in gear this time.

When he woke in Crumpsall hospital surrounded by the kindness of nurses Michael sensed something had to change. He couldn't just carry on by himself anymore and when he left the hospital he joined the cladiators, a group fighting to get money for the cladding to be replaced on apartment blocks around the city. In his joining with them he felt a sense of solidarity and realized he would no longer drink alone in the old man pubs he loved.

Back in work they had this professional development thing that he'd signed up for as a break from ghost allocations. It was up on the fifth floor, and he could see the ever-changing skyline of the city he'd come to as a horny student, so many moons ago. The two amiable presenters gave out a free book called *The Wiggly Career* that the session was going to be based on.

After the usual round of awkward introductions and too much information they were put into pairs with the person next to them and the person next to Michael was called Katja. They were all given these little strips of paper with lots of different words on and asked to put the words under three headings, *Matters Least, Matters Some, Matters*

Most, and when they'd agreed on the *Matters Most* list it looked like this:

> Kindness
> Fairness
> Trust
> Integrity
> Courage
> Authenticity
> Confidence
> Excellence
> Success

They were asked to discuss the results in terms of their careers, but Michael just listened as Katja talked about her daughter Nadia, and about the rising cost of nursery care, the rising cost of everything. Katja had an odd accent, Polish by way of Glasgow, but Michael had always liked women that were different. She wore white jeans and trainers and a pink jumper and had a gold, heart shaped necklace, and then there were her hands, the fingernails of which were painted a glittering pink.

After the course he went back to the office and looked her up on Teams but resisted messaging her straight away. Late in the day he got a message from her saying how much she'd enjoyed the course, and that she hoped he'd also found it useful. He replied back asking if he could buy her a drink in the pub after work.

They sat at the back of The Town Hall Tavern, at a table near the little flight of stairs and with a view of the alley. They could hear the clattering of building work in

Albert Square and the dull hum of yellow trams passing. Every time Michael looked at Katja he thought, fucking hell, she's well fit, and there was a kindness about her, and he looked longingly at her painted nails and her necklace and her pink jumper. They were holding hands under the table, and she stroked his fingers and he started getting a boner and when they kissed she tasted of strawberries.

He'd told Katja about the fire and she and Nadia came with him to a conference in St Peter's Square. The cladiators had got Labour's Andy Burnham on board, and he seemed like a great guy, but trying to get things changed felt like pissing in the wind. Michael always thought he'd stick with the cladiators, but when Katja got a job in Scotland they decided to get the fuck out of this sold out city.

Neighbours

I

Mrs Marwood was the oldest person I'd ever seen. If she ever needed any help with anything you would heard the *tap tap tap* of her stick on the wall and Mum would go round and help her with whatever it was she needed doing.

We had a garden fence made out of green painted wire and it was a bit like a goal and I had this little plastic brown ball like a mini football and I'd throw the ball against the red brick of the house and when it came back I'd head or volley it towards the goal which was on my left. Day and night I'd do this, sometimes knowing my Dad was watching from the bedroom window upstairs, and I'd try and impress him.

Quite often I'd head or volley the ball over the fence as it was only about three foot high, and I'd have to climb over the splintered green paint wooden bit at the top of the fence and jump into Mrs Marwood's garden to get the ball back. One time I did this and as I stood there I felt midges on my face and on my arms and on my bare legs, not biting Scottish ones just irritating Mancunian ones, and I stood there scratching. Then I heard our back door open and Dad popped his head out, the light from the kitchen flooding our garden right back towards the privet hedge that used to be there before the high fence. He was asking me to come in probably, and as I stood there looking at him I felt a cold hand on my shoulder. I turned and saw Mrs Marwood there, a ghost, about a hundred and fifty years old and with a goiter on her neck like a swollen nightmare. Before she could speak I jumped back over into my own garden, Dad laughing his head off. I left the ball behind and in the morning I saw it there on the grass, punctured.

2

I stood with one foot on the bog and one foot on the sink and could see out of the top part of the bathroom window, the bit that wasn't frosted. The mother and daughter from next door were sunbathing, just lying there with bikinis and sunglasses on. When I think back now they must have seen me.

3

This was when I lived in the high rise and this fucker lived next door to me and two doors down was my sister, and he went out with my sister ten years then broke her fucking heart. She stayed friends with him but when I got home pissed I'd bang on his door threatening to kick the shit out of him. My sister's never really spoke to me since then. But I remember, she was round my flat every night for about a month until she got over it. We're not the same kind of people. If someone fucks me over I hate them. Someone fucks my sister over I hate them too. Fuck all this staying friend's bollocks.

4

Wanky man wanks every morning and makes a lot of noise every time. Every single morning. I'm watching breakfast TV and there's this noise comes through the ceiling. Doesn't sound like pleasure. It sounds more like a painful shit. What gives it away is the sound of him scuttling over to the bathroom after he's shot his load.

5

Got a mortgage on an end terrace. Pretty quiet on one side.

Wolf

WOLF SEES THAT his pal has lost weight, uses the stick more and more, and he wells up a bit because Wolf's lost his dad recently and now every old person he knows, every time he sees an old person he knows, Wolf thinks it's the last time he'll see them, or might be the last time he'll see them, and so he watches his pal and already knows his pal will become a ghost, he'll come to this pub again, and all his pals, he'll see all his pals walking away as ghosts, and that's if the pub doesn't become a ghost first. The pub will become a ghost, like people become ghosts, like buildings become ghosts, like the place you live in becomes a ghost, and Wolf thinks he'll be a ghost himself soon enough and that he's always believed in ghosts. He's seeing one now, walking away. He can feel it.

Crumbs

H E REMEMBERS NOW how she used to moan about the toast crumbs, how she'd lift the sofa cushion up and show him how there were loads of crumbs on his side and none on her side. This went on for years. One time he grated the end of a loaf of stale bread and saved the crumbs in a little urn as a cheap alternative to grated cheese. He'd tried the breadcrumbs with a meal, and it wasn't great, so he went back to parmesan. But what he did with the remainder of the breadcrumbs one morning was lift up the sofa cushion and throw them all under it.

He remembered the scream. Then he heard her laughing and he got up and went to see her. It looked like she was dying from laughter, all doubled up on the floor and struggling to breathe. He'd loved to make her laugh, for years he made her laugh like that.

Raking in the Overtime

B Y THE GATE there's a bare tree with brambles under it, and the brambles are filled with faded crisp packets and beer cans. There's an empty pint pot on a stretch of crumbling wall next to the shutter door of an industrial unit. Next to the shutter door there's a laminated bit of plastic drilled into the wall that says, IF NO ANSWER FROM BELL DELIVER AT FRONT DOOR. There's the stale smell of piss, a scattering of silver canisters on the ground. Up above, on the corrugated roof, CCTV cameras record fuck all.

Arriving just as it gets light, Steve gets out of his idling Aygo, fishes the key out of his pocket and fiddles with the freezing padlock. He swings open the gates, gets back in the Aygo and drifts in slowly over the speed bump, parking just to the side of the shutter door.

It's Sunday morning, and a road normally clogged with lorries and cars is silent. A seagull moans high above. Steve likes this quiet, loves his Sunday morning, there's fuck all on the M60 and he rakes in the overtime. He unfurls the red shutter on the front door, opens the door itself, then drags the shutter closed behind him again. He's got stuff to do, there's loads of orders come in, the month before Christmas is their peak time.

First of all, he goes and turns on the oil heater by his workbench, then he goes to the little kitchen, fills the kettle and puts it on. The instant coffee has gone a bit solid in the jar so he bangs the jar on the table, loosens the coffee up and then spoons a tablespoon of coffee into a Bolton Wanderers cup that could do with bleaching.

The radio is shit on a Sunday morning so he connects his phone to the stereo on the shop floor and plays his Spotify playlist, which he's called Sunday Morning Coming Down. It's mainly Irish folk music, he loves it. *On Raglan Road* is the first one on it, ringing out across the empty industrial unit.

He looks at what he left himself the day before. Some old dear from Didsbury wants a frame around her grandson's graduation picture so he makes a start on that. As he does so, he hears a hammering and banging on the shutter door. This has never happened before.

What do you want? he shouts.

There's another bang on the shutter.

Look stop banging on the fucking shutter and let me open it.

He opens the shutter and there's a lad standing there, shivering. Looks about thirty and shouts, I need your bog mate!

For fuck's sake. Okay just come in. It's on your left down there.

The lad stinks of booze, but what can you do? More than once Steve has parked up on a Sunday morning and seen a big pile of shit. He's seen this lad before, wandering around near the petrol station.

Five minutes or so later the lad comes back. Thanks mate, look I appreciate it.

It's fine. If you've got to go you've got to go. I'd rather you bang on my door than shit on my doorstep.

Thank you, thank you, I really appreciate it.

No problem.

I'm sorry to be cheeky mate, but you can't spare a few quid can you, he asks, still shivering.

Look, let me get you a coffee, you look freezing.

Nah, you're okay.

Look, sit down, says Steve, pulling a chair up near the oil heater. Sit there next to that heater and I'll make you a coffee.

He comes back with the coffee and the lad is nodding off in the chair. Steve notices how filthy the lad is. His jacket and trainers and trousers, even his woolly hat, they're all covered in muck, and the lad fucking stinks.

Wakey, wakey, get that down your neck.

Thanks mate, he says.

What's your name lad?

Kevin.

Good to meet you, Kevin. I'm Steve. What's the score? Haven't you got a toilet at home?

Nah.

You haven't got a toilet?

I live in a tent.

You live in a tent?

Yeah.

Whereabouts?

Can't say.

No worries, says Steve. I guess you don't want people to know where you are.

Yeah, something like that. Well I'm basically under the M60, you know just up there, near the river. I'm dry under the motorway bridge. It's a lifestyle choice.

Conversation Through a Letterbox

HOOKERS CALLED THROUGH it and it flapped on windy nights so I could hear it, but because it was council property and the door was thick and the letterbox had this cover on it, it wasn't too draughty. I also stuck a woolly hat in there. If ever any post got shoved through I could only hope it was an acceptance for a poem or a story. Back in those days you sent self-addressed envelopes so I knew as soon as I saw the envelope, even before seeing my own writing, that it was from some small literary magazine. If it was a rejection I would immediately screw it up and put it in the bin, blah blah fucking blah, whatever. If it was an acceptance then it really lifted me. I remember the first thing I ever had published was a poem and the acceptance came via one of my own envelopes and through the letterbox up on the seventh floor of that shithole council block, and that morning I strutted out of my flat and strode down the road feeling a foot taller, a published poet, not like all the fucking plebs around me.

Otters

HE PICKED UP a copy of *Tarka the Otter* from the Children's Society bookshop and as he read it his mind kept drifting back to the time when, as a young man, he was sexually awakened by an older woman researching her own book on otters.

He was on holiday and had been swimming in the sea on the day he met her. Later she said that made him smell like an otter and that was why she wanted to fuck him.

They got chatting in the hotel. All the time she was looking into his eyes. She was forever stretching her back and sticking her chest out. They went up to her room and he took her from behind and grabbed her tits and came very quickly, saying *fucking hell* in frustration as she laughed.

A few months later she drove three hundred miles to see him and they shagged on the couch in front of the window of the ground floor studio flat he lived in at the time. He lasted longer as she dangled her swingers in the window before soaking his dick with her come. Later she sat on the couch and he gently pushed his dick in and out of her mouth before coming all over her smiling face. The following morning, he woke up with her giving him a blow job. She laughed and thanked him for breakfast.

High Rise

THESE FUCKING HIGH rise, what's that about, half empty fucking skyscrapers owned by rich cunts now, that's Manchester. Gentrification. Lost all it's fucking soul if you ask me. Build a load of fucking skyscrapers so you look like a big city, twenty years ago there was fuck all skyscrapers but we was better off round here. Walk a few yards out of the city centre and you're in Hulme, shithole. The other way Collyhurst, shithole. Ardwick, shithole. I know they are shitholes cos I've lived there. I'm not a town planner, or some dick with a blog. Live in Chorlton-Upon-Medlock now. No fucker has even heard of this place. Chorlton Cum Hardy, yeah, but nobody calls it that. Fucking Chorltonia, less said about that place the better. Six quid for a fucking chai latte and some patronizing cunt in a woolly hat who did an advert once and thinks he's Tom Cruise. Craft beer and street food, don't get me started on that either, it's the biggest fucking con since bottled water.

Chorlton upon Medlock used to be great, and now they are going to put a load of fucking high rise up round here for the fucking students. Students all over the fucking place in this city, paying two grand a month for a shoebox.

There's no fucking community anymore though is there? Just the poor giving to the poor while the rich look out for the rich. What a bag of shite. And fucking politics is bollocks as well. Fucking Starmer, give me a fucking break. The morals on these cunts fucking stink. Two faced cunts the lot of them. I tell you something, and you might laugh, the only one I ever voted for was Corbyn. Corbs. Decent fucking bloke if you ask me, the only fucking decent one among the lot of them. And got shafted over supposed anti-semitism. What a fucking joke. But that's the fucking world we live in now, the black and white Gen Z fucking clown mob. Try two opposing ideas in your head at the same time you brain dead pricks.

Big Glass Houses,
For You and Me

THE HOUSE HAD been built in the 1940s and Kev thought, I'm going to get rid of all that brick and make the house out of glass instead, so he did and all through the house of his grand design light shone; it was light and airy, the air flowed through, not like in those horrible old buildings made of brick. Soon his neighbours started to copy him, so that where at first the glass houses stood out from the brick houses, soon the brick houses were standing out from the glass houses. The glass houses towered above the remaining brick houses, and every new glass house had to be bigger than the glass house before it, and the Manhattan of glass houses continued to grow and grow. But this was Tameside, not Manhattan. The old Roker Park estate, once a mix of terraced and semi-detached brick houses, had now become a glistening collection of airy glass buildings. All of the ordinary people were rich now and never saw each other again, except through the glass. In the lap of luxury, Kev sat in his hot tub, staring through the window and stoned off his tits on ket, and his mind drifted to old Mrs Grace, who had been his next-door neighbour for many years. She would see him in the garden and come over and talk and he talked back to her, standing there for ages nattering over the garden fence. Although she was old she was interesting and had stories. He could tell she was lonely and wanted to talk and he did talk to her, but not with any pity, more in the hope that someone would do that for him one day when he was old. After thinking about that he got up and went out to his smoothly gravelled driveway and picked up armfuls of stones and took them back inside. Walking up the tangerine staircase he threw gravel at the sunset windows until his arm ached and the blemished glass glinted in the starlight.

The Chief Thing About This Game, Chief

THE CHIEF THING about this game, chief, is to just make it look like you're online all the time. I put a fork on the keys and that makes it look like I'm on Teams. I re-pointed all of my fucking outside wall yesterday, most of it anyway. And two hours for lunch I usually have. If anyone messages you on Teams the worst thing to do is answer right away. That's a sure sign you're doing fuck all. You with me, chief?

The Embankment

THE GOODS TRAIN passed and he could see the driver in there all relaxed and alone, sitting back and it seemed maybe he was reading a newspaper but that couldn't have been right you couldn't drive a train while reading a newspaper. It looked good though, being a train driver. The train passed and the carriages went past, on and on, and each one of them said HOPPER on the side and the train just kept going, quite slowly now, and there was an empty bit where one of the carriages had been. It was like he could have just calmly stepped over onto it and it was amazing. How did the driver know what was going on at the back of the train? Maybe it would be good to be a train driver when he grew up.

The other thing he sometimes did on the embankment was collect loads of blackberries from all the prickly bushes, collect them all in a big plastic tub his mum gave him. He'd take them home and she'd make a pie out of them that they had with custard. He liked it although he had to put sugar on them because the blackberries tasted so strong. Sometimes he had to squint his eyes to eat them.

Another day he's walking over the brick bridge along

the back path that goes alongside the embankment by the railway. He can see from up on the bridge over to the side of the embankment where a group of kids are sitting in pairs and kissing each other. The sight of that makes him feel a bit funny but he walks closer and he can see Nicola, one of the girls from next door, and she's snogging this lad from Woodbridge Avenue called Haaland Baguley. There's other kids there and he recognizes their faces when they stop snogging and he watches between the grey wires of the embankment fence as they swop over with each other, so that they are all snogging someone else. After a bit Nicola sees him watching and she laughs and tells him to climb over the fence and go over to her. She asks him if he has ever kissed a girl and does he want to, and he says nothing and she asks him if he wants to kiss her, and he says nothing again and he's just sitting on the grass of the embankment opposite her. He can feel all the other kids watching and feels his face going red and someone shout's ha, he's gone all red, and just then he kisses Nicola on the lips. It wasn't how everyone else was kissing, but yeah, he kissed her on the lips, then he ran off down the embankment and climbed back over the wire fence. He could feel his face all red and something about it was weird.

He kept walking down the back path until he got nearer to the road bridge. Under that road bridge there was a big tree with a rope swing under it, a rope tied to one of the high branches, and then at the end of the rope there was a stick. He went down the embankment and took hold of the rope and walked back up the hill with it, then put the stick under his legs and clung on to the rope and lifted his legs and went flying out on the swing so that it was like he was almost over the railway line. When he got off the swing, slipping a bit on the soil, he went over to some blackberries and picked some of them and stuffed a few in his mouth before gobbing them out and leaving a big blob of purple on the soil. After that he went back down the hill and sat right near the railway lines and then he went into the bushes by himself. He started rubbing himself like he'd been doing before, and it felt so nice but this time there was something weird. Where like before he did it, it felt dead nice, and just stopped feeling nice, and nothing else happened, this time he did it and felt a surge of something like nothing before. When it all came flying out he was thinking, fucking hell, what's this!

Acknowledgements

Thanks once again to Chris, Jen and all the team at Salt. Thanks also to Alan McMunnigall, whose online writing class thi wurd is the dog's bollocks.

Some of these stories first appeared (in slightly different form and some with different titles) in *Fictive Dream*, *Flash: The International Short Short Story Magazine*, *Litro*, *Spelk*, *Strands Lit Sphere*, and *The Common Breath*. My thanks to the editors.

This book has been typeset by
SALT PUBLISHING LIMITED
using Granjon, a font designed by George W. Jones
for the British branch of the Linotype
company in the United Kingdom. It has been
manufactured using Holmen Book Cream
65gsm paper, and printed and bound by Clays
Limited in Bungay, Suffolk, Great Britain.

CROMER
GREAT BRITAIN
MMXXV